STOP KICKING THE LION

Randall Probert

Stop Kicking the Lion

by Randall Probert

www.randallprobertbooks.net
email: randentr@megalink.net

Art and Photography credits:

Cover photo, chest, from iStockphoto.com
and sunburst from 123RF.com

Author's photo on back cover by Patricia Gott

Disclaimer
This book is a work of fiction,
although there are some historical facts included.

ISBN: 979-8422592272

Printed in the United States of America

Published by
Randall Enterprises
P.O. Box 862
Bethel, Maine 04217

Acknowledgments

I would like to thank Laura Ashton of Woodland Georgia, for her help formatting this book for printing. And I would also like to thank Amy Henley of Newry, Maine, for her help typing this, for the rewrites and her advice.

More Books by Randall Probert

CHAPTER 1

The wind was beginning to blow stronger, and the waves were tossing Enig McFarney in his fishing boat too much. He had had a successful day fishing in the North Atlantic two miles out from Greenock Bay in Scotland. If he had timed his return correctly, the tide coming in would carry him swiftly up the bay to the fish market on Greenock's harbor.

As he turned his sail to turn into the bay, he could feel the incoming tide carrying him along. This trip he had caught mostly haddock with a few cod.

Enig was only seventeen and he had graduated from school a month earlier. Ever since he was big enough to work, he had worked six days a week after school and during the summers in his father's boat building shop. So, too, had his older brother Fergus.

At eighteen, Fergus had left the boat building business for a career in the Scottish Army. Enig was more like his father, and he loved fishing, the ocean and building fishing boats.

While Fergus took after his mother, Hilda; taller than his father and Enig, and slim, he was also smart as a whip. Enig resembled his father, Eachann, more. Five foot ten, barrel chested and stocky and stronger than a mule, like his father.

Enig had always dreamed of sailing across the Atlantic to the new world. He was tired of the Crown's domination and every shilling he earned was put in the bank. *Someday I'll have me enough to follow my dream.*

He pulled up to the fish market's wharf and pulled in his sail and secured his boat and began carrying his catch up to the scales.

"You have a good catch this trip, Master Enig. I'll pay you one pound and four shillings."

Enig thanked him and then, using oars, he rowed up to his father's wharf, only a short distance away.

Enig worked six days a week in the boat shop for his father and on Sundays he went fishing.

At the supper table that evening, his father asked, "How was your catch today, son?"

"It was good. Mr. Croft paid me a pound and four shillings."

"That is a good day's catch. Son, you know when you turn eighteen, you'll be required to serve in Scotland's military."

"Yes."

"I would like you to enlist into the Scottish Navy and get some shipboard and sailing experience. Then after three years, I'd like you to come back and help with the business.

"Your brother, Fergus, has no interest in the business, so when I'm gone, the business will be yours. With this experience you'll be more valuable to the business. And it will do you good to get out and see some of the world."

There was no argument from Enig. At least this way, part of his dream would come true. "This week I'll walk over to the navy yard and talk with someone."

* * *

After eating supper, Enig changed his clothes and walked the short distance to see his childhood sweetheart, Innis Craig.

The sun didn't set in Greenock, Scotland, until after 10 p.m., so the two went for a walk on the boardwalk, which soon led to the highlands just behind the city.

The hills were covered with a low growing brush and trails winding through the bushes and hillside, worn deep into the soil from generations of people walking the hill country.

"Sometime this week, Innis, I'm going to talk with someone at the navy port about enlisting."

"We knew as soon as you turned eighteen, you'd be required to serve three years. Then after the three years maybe we can get married," Innis said.

"We will," that's all Enig said.

On top of the highest hill, they sat down on a bench overlooking Greenock. They sat there in silence for a few minutes looking over the city and enjoying that day's warm sunshine.

"It's 10 o'clock, Innis, and if we wait any longer, we'll have to walk back in the dark."

"Let's go," Innis said.

They stood up and embraced and kissed hungrily for a long few minutes. "Let's go," she said.

"What will you do, Innis, while I'm gone?"

"When school starts again, I already have a job helping Mrs. Stanley with the younger school children. Until then, I go to work tomorrow in the restaurant for Mr. and Mrs. Darrow."

There was only a bright halo from the sun over the horizon now, as they kissed again and said goodnight.

* * *

At breakfast the next morning, his mother, Hilda, asked, "How is Innis, Enig?"

"We both wish we could marry now instead of waiting until I finish my service obligation."

"Well, the fire will burn hotter until you can," Eachann smiled.

"When you leave, son, I'll have to hire two more men to take your place. There is another order coming in on Wednesday. That puts us three boats ahead."

Enig heard and understood what his father was trying to say without having to come right out with it. He would have to hire two men to replace him. It was a compliment.

The McFarney boat building business had a good reputation

among the offshore fishermen, and the business was making good money. It had taken eight years to create the reputation and to finally be making money.

There were several years when business was slow, and Eachann had to make up for lost wages by fishing. He enjoyed fishing but he wanted the boat building business to provide better for his family.

Eachann and Enig went to work and Hilda picked up breakfast makings and then did laundry. She understood serving three years in the navy would be good experience for Enig, but she still would miss her son.

She had no idea when they would see their oldest son, Fergus. She knew he had spent some time in the colonies but she was sure he was back in England again. And she knew they would never see their daughter again. Especially after the harsh words between Blair and her father. She had run off with an army lieutenant to London. Neither of her folks wanted her to go. Then Eachann had exploded with anger, telling his daughter what he thought of the English and now his own daughter was running off with a lieutenant. To Eachann this was unforgivable and he had said, "You leave here with that damned Brit then you'll never be welcomed back."

It was bad enough that Fergus had joined the damned Red Coats, but no daughter of mine is going to marry one!

Hilda loved her husband, but she later admonished him for what he had said to their daughter. She doubted if she would ever see Fergus or Blair again. And for that she could not forgive him.

* * *

Enig went about his job at the boat shop like he did every day, except there were intervals when he would think about joining the navy and sailing to new lands and places. He was actually beginning to look forward to enlisting, and dreaming where his travels would take him.

"Enig, Enig. You must keep your mind on your job, son," Eachann said. He realized Enig was thinking about the navy. He turned away and smiled.

"How are the planks doing in the jig?" Eachann asked.

"They should be ready to take out by evening."

"Then we might as well leave them until morning."

"By then the planks we have in the steamer will be ready to put in the jig," Enig replied.

Two years earlier, Enig had talked with his dad about preforming the planks and letting them dry while in a jig. Once the planks were dry, they were preformed to fit the ribs on the boat they were building.

This made production easier with fewer broken planks. And it took less time to plank the boat now than how they had been doing it. The idea was Enig's but Eachann had the ability to build the steamer and jig.

Eachann had kept the jig secret from other boat builders and he was well known for building the best fishing boats.

* * *

Enig took the horse and buggy to the Naval Base in Port Glasgow. "What can I do for you, young man?" Lieutenant Dow asked.

"I would like to talk about enlisting."

"How old are you?"

"Seventeen, I'll be eighteen June thirteenth."

"From your stature, I would have said you were older. Any particular reason for choosing the Navy and not the infantry?"

"Yes, I like boats. I work with my father building fishing boats. I have my own fishing boat. And I'd like to see something besides Greenock, Scotland."

"Those are all good reasons. Can you be at the Naval Base on July 1st?"

"Yes, Sir, I surely can."

"Be there before 0800. And good luck."

Before leaving, he had to fill out a form explaining his educational level and his work experience. Then he was free to leave.

Before going home, he stopped at Craig's Restaurant for a cup of tea and to talk with Innis.

"I talked with Lieutenant Dow today at the Navy Base in Port Glasgow. I'm to report to the base in Glasgow on July 1st."

"I guess we knew this was coming but I'll surely miss you, Enig."

* * *

The next day Eachann started advertising for two men to replace Enig. Two days later, two young men with families were hired, Peter Canon and Boyd Carr. Carr actually had some experience working for a repair company in Glasgow and Canon had recently finished his three years in the Navy. He had spent most of his indenture in the carpentry shop on the Glasgow Base, repairing her majesty's fleet ships.

Both Enig and his father thought they both would be good workers.

Enig pulled his boat from the water and secured it in an empty shed behind the shop. He spent most evenings and Sundays with Innis. He wanted to spend as much time with her as he could. The Navy Base was not far away, but Enig was hoping to sail.

CHAPTER 2

Early the morning of July 1ˢᵗ, Enig said goodbye to his mother and Innis, and his dad drove him to the base in Port Glasgow. "Have fun, son, and remember to do whatever you are asked to do by your superiors and always do your best, son.

"I have no idea if or when you'll be granted any leave time, but come home when you can. And don't forget to write."

"Thanks, Dad, and I'll be fine."

Eachann turned the buggy around and headed for home. Enig walked through the gates and was met by a security guard who gave him directions to the induction hall.

There were only twelve new recruits there and all of them were of Enig's age. There would only be three weeks of training and then each would be stationed elsewhere.

Two days after his arrival, Scotland's prized ship, the *Queen Mary,* arrived for refitting and annual repairs. Two days later, Lieutenant Burns was reviewing the new recruit's enlistment papers and he recognized the name McFarney and he wondered if this young man was a family member of the boat building company.

"Ensign," Lieutenant Burns said.

"Yes, Sir?"

"Find the new recruit McFarney and have him brought to my office immediately."

"Yes, Sir," and the ensign left and he returned only minutes later with Enig McFarney.

"Sir, Seaman McFarney."

"Thank you, Ensign. Dismissed."

Enig was still standing at attention in front of the lieutenant's desk. He had learned that much.

"At ease, seaman. Is it your family who builds fishing boats?"

"Yes, Sir, McFarney."

"Your family builds extraordinary fine boats. I'm assuming that is where you were working before joining the Scottish Navy."

"Yes, Sir," and then he added, "I've worked in my father's shop ever since I was big enough to carry hull planks."

"Seaman, would you prefer to stay ashore and work in our shops repairing ships or would you prefer duty aboard one of Her Majesty's ships?"

Enig was quick to reply. "I would prefer shipboard duty, Sir."

"Good, that is what I wanted to hear. Bosun MacCangus aboard the *Queen Mary* is retiring after her next voyage to Nova Scotia and the colonies. With your experience with building fishing boats, you will make an excellent candidate for a bosun's apprentice.

"Then when Bosun MacCangus leaves the *Queen Mary,* with the captain's approval, you'll be promoted to bosun. The choice is yours and I need your answer now."

"Hell yes, Sir!"

The lieutenant overlooked Enig's enthusiasm. "I see that you have only recently turned eighteen. Most of the crew will be older than you with more time at sea. You're a big stocky-looking fella. You'll have to be able to supervise men as well as knowing how to do the work yourself. Will this be a problem for you, seaman?"

"No, Sir. Not at all."

"Okay, finish today on whatever you were doing and

tomorrow after breakfast report to Bosun MacCangus."

"Yes, Sir."

"Dismissed."

For the rest of that day, Enig was excited beyond belief. The officers were treating him with much respect. He was doing what he enjoyed and knew best, and he would be going to sea much sooner than he had anticipated. No, life couldn't be much better.

* * *

Enig hurried through his breakfast and rushed over to the slip where the *Queen Mary* was tied up. He had never been this close to one of those tall sailing ships before. He was struck by its beauty and streamlined appearance.

"She's a beauty ain't she, laddie," a voice said behind him.

"She sure is."

"You must be young McFarney."

"Yes ,Sir, I am, Seaman Enig McFarney reporting for duty."

"I'm not a *sir*. That is saved for the gentlemen sailors. I am the *bosun*. The top-ranking member of the deck workers. When the crew or officers are present you will address me as Bosun. When we are alone, it's Fraser.

"You look awful young to be taking my place when I go ashore. But you're a husky lad. I hope you can handle men.

"There's no fight'n aboard ship. If you have a problem with some seaman you take it to the captain. Always. If you want the crew to respect and work for ya, then you'll have to earn their respect."

"Yes, Bosun, I'll remember that."

"Well come aboard and I'll introduce you to the crew. The officers are all on shore leave."

"What repairs are being done, Bosun?"

"The center main mast developed a crack and we'll have to replace it, and while we're at it, we'll replace those sails and the rope rigging. Getting the mast down and erecting the new one will take about three days. Rigging her with new sails and ropes will take another week.

"The rudder will also be inspected. That shouldn't be a problem. We replaced that a year ago."

"It sounds like a lot of work, Bosun."

"It is, laddie."

"Is this a man of war ship? I see she carries cannons."

"No—she's no man of war, although there are six five-pound cannons."

"What class of a sailing ship is she, Bosun?"

"She's faster than a man of war and although she carries six cannons, she is used mostly for supplying the Crown's forts and outpost. We also carry mail and messages for the admiralty and officers occasionally to an outpost."

"Did you ever fight in any sea battles?"

"Yes, a Spanish man of war had fired on us and missed and we returned fire with the two port cannons and chipped her main mast, and we were able to sail off. The Spanish captain probably figured we were an easy target. But Captain Gordon Graham knew his stuff and showed the Spanish captain we were nobody to fool with. He fired a few shots at us but nothing came close.

"The *Queen Mary* is a fine ship, laddie. Come on, we better get aboard and get to work.

"Today we dismantle the rigging and sails from the center mast. For now, I want you with me."

"Yes, Sir—oh, Bosun."

Before beginning work, the bosun introduced the crew to Enig. Then he said, "Come on, laddies, let's get those sails down."

By noon the crew had the center mast sails down and rolled up and sitting on the dock. "Good work, men. This afternoon we will free the mast from the stanchel and hook up the block and tackle and ropes, to lower it gentle."

"Bosun, what do we anchor the block and tackle to, to

lower the mast?"

"We'll hook the aft and forward port anchors together and winch 'em until we have a tight anchor chain, and then lock both winches and hook the block and tackle to the chain.

"After lunch that'll be our job," Bosun said.

* * *

The anchor chains were hooked together and winched tight. "Let's go below, Enig, and see how the boys are coming with releasing the mast."

Down below, "Harry,"—the boss—"what's the hold up? I thought you'd have this free by now," Bosun said.

"Bosun, there was so much wear in the lock we have had a difficult time to move it. We had to get two jacks from the shop and literally lift the mast back into position before we could remove the locks. We just now have the locks free and ready to drive them out."

"Continue, Harry. We'll just watch."

"If I understand you, Bosun, you plan to winch this mast out and then the new one back in," Enig said.

"That's right."

"That seems like a lot of unnecessary work. It would be like hitting your own hand with a hammer to get out of work."

"Do you have a better way of doing this?" Bosun asked.

"I might."

"Well?"

"Well you cut the mast in two pieces and put one piece in at a time. It would be easier and quicker."

"Go on." He now had everyone's attention.

"You cut the mast so the bottom portion is four feet above deck. I need paper and pencil to draw it out, so you'll see what I'm talking about."

"Eddie, go get us some paper and pencil."

Eddie ran off the ship and across the yard to the office. He was back in five minutes. "Here, Enig."

15

"Okay, you cut away half of the mast on both ends and splice them together. The two pieces will slide together," and he drew it out on the paper. "Then you bore holes in these places here and then you bolt the splice together. Then you soak some rope to get it pliable and stretch it. Then wrap the mast binding with the rope as tight as you can possibly wrap it. When the rope dries it will tighten against the mast."

"I see what you are saying. Have you ever done this before?"

"I helped my dad repair a cracked mast once on a ship and this is how we did it.

"If the locks were not worn out so much, all we would have to do is cut the scarves and slide the top on."

"I tell you what, Enig. The new mast is in the shop and the keyway lock has already been made in the butt end. Take as many men as you need and start work on it."

Bosun and three men went up on deck to start rigging the block and tackle and the others remained below to finish preparing for the new mast.

Before making any cuts, Enig drew out the lines on the new mast. Then he checked and rechecked his measurements. "Before we make any cuts, I want to sleep on it."

After supper that evening, Bosun went to talk with the base commander and tell him about Enig's new way of replacing the center mast. "It all sounds good, Bosun. Do you think he can do it?" the commander asked.

"He drew out the splice and how it would have to be done. Yes, I believe it'll work."

"Okay, Bosun, but I want you to oversee the procedure."
"Yes, Sir."

* * *

Before going to sleep that night, Enig drew up a clearer plan for making the splice. So the next morning in the shop he began by sighting down the length of the mast, for any defects or curvatures. There were no defects, but he and his two helpers rolled the mast because of a slight curve.

Then they measured where the mast was to be cut into two sections. Before cutting, they had to put supports under both ends. Bosun came into the shop then. "We're about to make the first cut, Bosun," Enig said.

"Are you absolutely sure about this, Enig?"

"Yes, Bosun, absolutely."

"Okay, Greg and Gavin, you two make the cut and I'll watch. Follow the line exactly."

"Okay, boss man," Greg said.

"If this works, it'll save us many hours of work," Bosun said.

Enig replied, "Of course it'll work."

"I wonder why we never thought of it before?"

"What about the bolts and nuts, Bosun?"

"How long do you need them?"

"Twenty-six inches from inside the head to the end of the threaded bolt."

"How many?"

"Six."

"I'd better go over to the blacksmith shop. He may have to make them."

By the time Bosun was back they had the mast in two pieces. "Smithy had four all made up. He'll get right on the other two.

"You have things under control here, Enig? I'm going to check on the other crew."

They worked on the bottom piece of the mast first. One saw blade cut to the center of the mast and then they turned it so they could make the next cut along the mast length; with the grain. This cut took a little longer. But when they had finished Enig was pleased with it.

They did the other piece next, "Just like the first one,

fellas."

This one had two high spots that Enig had to smooth out with a jack plane. "There, let's fit 'em together and see what we have."

Greg and Gavin brought the bottom part of the mast into position and while they were doing that Enig wrapped his arms around the top piece and pulled it into the other one. "It fits pretty good, fellas. Greg, you mark the center of the mast on top and Gavin you find a hammer and two nails and I'll find the center on the other end."

When that was done, they strung a line between the two nails. They only had to make one slight adjustment and the mast was now straight and the splice was a good, even fit.

* * *

With the center mast secured with a tight fit in place the men began assembling the rigging with new ropes and sails. This took more time than replacing the mast. By the end of that week the *Queen Mary* was refitted and cleaned and supplied with new equipment and food stores.

"Well, our part is done, laddie. Now we wait around the base until Captain Slaugo has orders to take her out. You excited about taking your first voyage, laddie?"

"I sure am."

"Laddie, you have proven you know your way around ship rigging and repairs, but you'll have to learn how to handle men. Good, hard-working men hate a weak-minded boss. But if you're too stern and rough, they just might throw you overboard. You'll have to learn to walk between the two. I'll help you as much as I can but in the end, it'll have to come from you."

"I understand, Bosun."

"You sure are big and strong enough. The laddies are still talking about your strength after you man handled that top piece of the center mast. I don't think any of them would be foolish enough to attack you. But if you abuse your rank, they just might team up to teach you a lesson or two.

"Most seamen are friendly and good natured but don't ever cross one, laddie."

"I'll remember, Bosun."

* * *

Some of the *Queen Mary* ordinary seamen were given a three-day leave. Bosun, Enig and a handful of others spent this time cleaning, polishing and making any repairs they found; stem to stern.

The *Queen Mary,* sitting high and proud, tied up to the docks at Port Glasgow, sure was a smart looking ship. Enig couldn't wait until she sailed.

CHAPTER 3

The day after the three-day leave, Captain Slaugo walked up the gangway. Bosun saw the captain first and said, "Captain on board. Attention!"

Everyone scurried to the main deck at attention. "I want to see this new mast, Bosun."

"Yes, Captain."

"Hmm, the base commander told me about this new idea and I had to see it for myself. The commander also said the idea was from a new seaman. I would like to see him, Bosun mate."

"Yes, Sir. Seaman McFarney, come forward."

Enig stopped and saluted and remained at attention. "At ease, seaman. Where did you come up with this idea?"

"From my father, Sir. Eachann McFarney. I helped him replace a similar mast once."

"I understand you'll be sailing as an apprentice for Bosun mate MacCangus."

"Yes, Sir."

"That's all, Seaman McFarney," Enig returned.

"Gentlemen, we set sail in three days. Starting at 0800 tomorrow, we will begin loading supplies for our base in Halifax, Nova Scotia, then to some of our ports along the east coast of the colonies.

"Three days from now, we'll be leaving at 0400 with the outgoing tide.

"The ship appears to be in good shape. Carry on."

Captain Slaugo left and the men went back to work.

After supper that night, Enig wrote long letters to his mom and dad and Innis. He had wanted to ask the commander for time to go home and see his family, but being a new recruit, he didn't suppose that would be quite proper. So he wrote his letters.

* * *

Twelve hours before they were to depart, the three lieutenants came aboard with their gear.

Captain Slaugo arrived in time for supper and before supper was served, he introduced his three officers. "Gentlemen, I'd like to take a moment and introduce my three officers: My First Officer and acting executive officer, Lieutenant Leslie David. My second officer, Lieutenant James Coburn and my third officer, Lieutenant Hew McFee.

"We are scheduled for departure at 0400. After supper, I want the rigging set to sail at 0400, not a minute later. I want to go out with the tide.

"Enjoy your meal and get what rest you can."

Enig lay down in his bunk but he was too excited to sleep. Bosun—well, he was snoring rather loudly. There were many images floating through his thoughts. Places he would see, the experience of crossing the Atlantic Ocean and visiting Nova Scotia and the Colonies. And, of course, his folks and Innis.

At exactly 0300 Bosun woke up and got out of bed, "You asleep, Enig?"

"No."

"Let's see if there is any hot tea in the galley."

Much to Enig's surprise the entire crew was there, and the cook had two steaming hot kettles of tea.

"When the Captain gives the okay, you and I will make sure the sails are set properly. Second Lieutenant Coburn will oversee the process. The captain more 'n likely will be at the helm directing helm maneuvers and the First Lieutenant will direct the settings of the sail and which sails to be used.

At 0400, Lieutenant David gave the order to Second Lieutenant Coburn. "Lieutenant Coburn, set sails. Bosun, have your men release the ropes to shore and pull them onboard."

There was only a gentle wind, but that was enough to fill the sails and the *Queen Mary* silently sailed away from Port Glasgow and the base towards the open ocean.

The sun rises early in northern Scotland in July and the *Queen Mary* had clear sailing all day. Then the ocean became rough and for three days they sailed in the rough, turbulent water.

"This is much rougher, Bosun, than I would have imagined it to be," Enig said.

"That's because we are crossing the North Atlantic current. When we get out of the current, it won't be so rough."

"How fast are we traveling now, Bosun?"

"Oh, it's hard to say for sure. Probably somewhere between fourteen and eighteen knots. Once we leave the current our speed will pick up a little. Then when we reach the Labrador current we'll pick up a couple more knots. You see that current flows south, not like the North Atlantic current. When we return to Scotland we'll stay in the North Atlantic current all the way back."

On the fourth day they finally sailed into calmer seas. All of the crew, except for the officers, had to stand a four-hour watch, either at the helm or forward on the bow as lookout. Enig's turned every third day. He especially enjoyed the helm duty, as this gave him some time to talk with Lieutenant McFee.

"Lieutenant."

"Yes."

"I understand why someone must man the lookout. But why way out here in the middle of the ocean?"

"Well, there's a small possibility of sighting a Spanish or French man of war. Right now, the Crown is not on even terms with either country. We are only a day and a half from the Labrador current and this time of year, huge icebergs travel south from Greenland. Need I say any more?"

"No, Sir, Lieutenant."

When Enig was assigned to bow lookout, he enjoyed this time alone. It gave him the only time alone there was to think about his mother and father and Innis. He missed them all, but he was not homesick.

As soon as the *Queen Mary* entered the Labrador current, Captain Slaugo told the commander, Lieutenant David, to set his course at 190°. That morning the bow lookout spotted the first iceberg, and it was huge. "As grand as that one is, laddie, it just might float right down to the colonies. That surely is a big piece of ice," Bosun said.

"One more week, laddie, or a bit less, we'll reach Halifax. Once the ship is secured, the captain usually gives us the night ashore—course we have to unload the supplies first."

One evening as Enig and Bosun were on the bow lookout, Enig said, "I'm surprised we didn't see any whales, Bosun."

"This time of year, you have to be where the whales are. More'n likely they all are to the north of here feeding. On our next trip we'll probably see some going south to warmer waters for the winter."

"I wonder how deep the water is here?" Enig asked.

"I do not know. But one thing is for certain, you couldn't hold your breath long enough to swim to the bottom, laddie.

"We're getting close to land, laddie. I be seeing birds in the air all day."

"It'll seem good to stand on dry land again."

"Aye, that it will, laddie."

* * *

At noon the next day, the *Queen Mary* pulled into the navy base's dock and the ship was tied off secure. The deck hands immediately began unloading the cargo for the base. With shore leave coming, the crews were not long unloading the supplies.

"There, laddie, we're done for the day. Let's say you and

me go ashore and find us a tavern where we can have us a steak and a pint of beer or two."

They found a tavern close to the base and had a steak and a couple pints of beer. Enig had never drank beer before and he wasn't sure he liked the taste. But he drank along with Bosun so not to hurt his feelings.

In the morning, he woke up with a hangover and thirsty. He was glad the ship was tied up at shore and not rolling and yawing over the ocean swells. One lesson learned.

For two days, Captain Slaugo was in conference with the base commander. The crews kept themselves busy cleaning the ship of caked-on salt brine and barnacles. "Bosun, what do you suppose the captain and commander are talking about?" Enig asked.

"Last night after you returned to the ship after supper, I was talking with a couple fellas who work in a fishery cannery, and they were telling me that the colonies are not happy with so much British control. Maybe there's more to it and that's what the captain and commander are talking about.

"How come you returned to the ship so early?"

"Oh, two pints was enough for me."

* * *

Once the captain finished his talks with the base commander on the third day, he brought back with him documents for London and for the navy base in Boston.

"Something is going on, Bosun."

"What do you mean, Enig?"

"The captain and commander talked for two days and when he returns he's carrying a valise full of papers."

"It may have something to do with what I heard in the tavern two nights ago, about the American colonies upset with British domination," Bosun said.

"I can understand that, but I think there's more to it."

"Maybe, but take my advice, laddie, and stay out of it."

"But aren't you curious, Bosun?"

"Stay out of it, laddie."

* * *

Before leaving Halifax, the *Queen Mary* replenished her food stores with fresh fish, ham, eggs and garden vegetables.

With food stores replenished they set sail late that evening as the tide was going out. "From here, laddies, we go to Boston. Boston is much bigger than Halifax and taverns and girls line the waterfront. It's a pretty good port, laddie."

"Where will we go from Boston?"

"Probably New Haven, Connecticut, across the sound from New York's Long Island. From there to Charleston, South Carolina. From Charleston, we sometimes go to the Caribbean. But I doubt if we'll make the trip this time. This time of year, there are some God-awful blows off Cape Hatteras, North Carolina. I've seen me swells there, laddie, taller than the center mast on the *Queen Mary*. It ain't no fun, laddie. Trust me. Many a ship and good men have been lost to that terrible stretch of water.

"It's too bad we don't make the trip this time. The captain always buys a barrel of Jamaican rum for the men. On the voyage home he allows one glass a day with evening meal. The men they surely do appreciate it."

After leaving Halifax, the *Queen Mary* stayed away from the North current. "These waters here, laddie, is a grand ole fishery. Fishing boats come from a far ways to fish here. Come daylight, we'll probably see one or two.

"When I finish this trip, I just might pack up my wife and things and make the move to Nova Scotia or the territory of Maine. It would be a good life for retirement."

"Would your wife come?"

Bosun laughed then and said, "Well, if she don't I'd find me a pretty young Indian girl. Yes, sir, by cracky. It would be nice to have a young Indian girl to crawl into bed with and to warm up the sheets."

25

They both were quiet for a few minutes and then Bosun said, "Probably a young lad as yourself could make a good living fishing in these waters." Then he laughed and added, "Someone your age, laddie, could have his self two or three Indian girls."

* * *

When they tied up in Boston, a currier from Admiral Montie's office came aboard with a letter from the admiral. At the evening meal, Captain Slaugo addressed the men. "I received a letter today from Admiral Montie and he has requested that no one go off the base tonight. It seems as though the Colonies are petitioning the governor for less British rule and lower taxes. If any try to leave the base they will be stopped and turned around at the security gates. If any violate this request, you'll be put on bread and water in the hold. That's all."

"Laddie, when the Admiral makes a request, you might as well know it is an order. And trust me, you don't wanna be in the hold for a week on bread and water. It ain't pleasant. Trust me."

Bosun and Enig remained on the open deck near the bow after supper long into the night. About 10 o'clock they could hear a disturbance somewhere in the city and they heard two rifle shots. "I guess the Admiral wasn't kidding, laddie. I know we are in the Crown's Military, albeit the Scottish Navy, but I am inclined to sympathize with the colonists. The Crown cannot keep its nose out of the business of other countries and they are always fighting against someone, so why should these people have to pay heavy taxes to support the Crown and their affairs when they live on another continent.

"I think I just made up my mind, laddie. When I get home and retire, just as soon as I can I am packing up and moving to Nova Scotia whether my wife comes or not. Yes siree, laddie, that's what I'll be doing."

By the time they arrived in New Haven, the weather had become hot and humid. That first night, although the crew was allowed to go ashore, many chose to stay aboard on the open deck.

26

Some even chose to sleep in the somewhat cooler ocean breeze. After listening to Bosun talk about not wanting to live any longer under British rule and moving to Nova Scotia, he began to think about the possibility. He would have to convince Innis. But he still had the better part of three years to serve in the Scottish Navy. He decided for now he'd better put that idea out of his head.

Bosun and Enig went ashore for supper. They found a tavern two blocks from the base and they each had steak and two pints of beer. "We have to be back on-board, laddie, before 2100 hours. We'd better be on our way back."

From New Haven they made a quick one day stop at Port Chester, New York. And again Captain Slaugo returned from a meeting with the Governor Mayor with a portfolio of documents. "I sure would like to know what all those papers have to say," Bosun said.

From Port Chester they left for Charleston, South Carolina, at midnight, with the outgoing tide

"Why the change, Bosun?" Enig asked.

"It has to be because of the rumors we have heard in the taverns and all the documents the captain comes back carrying when he meets with the base commanders. Me thinks there is trouble brewing in the colonies, laddie."

* * *

Before leaving Charleston, they filled the food lockers with fresh citrus fruits and vegetables, and salt pork and ham.

"We'll eat good for a few days, laddie."

"Where to now, Bosun?"

"We're making an unprecedented stop in Belfast, Maine. The captain has orders to load two one hundred foot pine trees that'll be made into masts. They'll be some cumbersome to work around, but the northern colonies produce excellent stock for the tall masts.

"You'll like this port, laddie, these people are the friendliest folks from Halifax to Charleston. And when you go to a pub for a pint there is no one there wanting to punch your lights out. You'll see, laddie."

Bosun was making this Belfast seem like a heaven. And he had been right about the fighting in all of the other pubs, without exception; both he and Bosun were rugged, stalky men but neither one wanted to waste shore leave fighting.

Before leaving Charleston, Captain Slaugo had made a deal with a local merchant to have a barrel of Southern Whiskey delivered to the ship. And just as Bosun had said, each crew were allowed a teacup of whiskey each evening. Enig discovered this helped him to sleep, in spite of Bosun's snoring.

The crew liked the captain and his officers. The captain was a fair man. But if any seaman got out of line, he would deal with it immediately. No one talked harshly about any of the officers.

* * *

The winds were strong on the trip to Belfast and sometimes blowing in the wrong directions. Two days they were able to maintain eight knots but the rest of the voyage it was probably close to five. It took the *Queen Mary* ten days to make the trip.

As the deck hands were securing the ship, Enig took a deep breath of air. "I can smell the pine forests from here, Bosun."

"It smells good, doesn't it."

It was evening before the ship was secured properly; most of the crew left the ship before eating supper, even the captain. The XO, Lieutenant David, stayed onboard.

Instead of steak tonight, both Enig and Bosun decided on baked haddock, potato and green beans. "I was getting tired of steak," Enig said.

From there they found a waterfront pub and they had a couple of pints. Enig immediately noticed how friendlier these people were compared to their southern counterparts, even those in Halifax.

The next morning, they took on more supplies before the

two-hundred-foot mast stocks covered the hatch covers.

While the supplies were being loaded, horse teams brought the two pine-tree length logs to the dock.

After lunch the crew began the loading process. The winches first lifted the butt end up and let it rest midship and the forward winches lifted the small end and swung it toward the bow, all while the aft winches kept the butt end up off the deck, so it would swing easier. It took two hours to load that one and another two hours to load the next one.

"There'd be less weight if the shore crews would debark them," Bosun said.

"Then, Bosun, without the bark, as the wood dried it would crack. The bark keeps a tight girth on the wood."

"I just learned something, laddie."

The crews would wait to lash them down securely until the next morning.

That evening, Enig had the clam chowder and Bosun had steak again. Along with their two pints.

"You know, Bosun, Belfast is a nice port. I could live here. I think."

* * *

The tide was due to go out at 1400 hours and at breakfast Lieutenant David said, "Men, I want the rigging set and sails already to go up at 1400 hours."

It was Bosun and Enig's job to secure the two pine logs and they were finished before 1000 hours. Then they helped with the rigging and sails.

At exactly 1400 hours the tide started to flow out, the sails were set and the *Queen Mary* slowly pulled away from the dock and Belfast.

The wind was now in their favor and by midnight the *Queen Mary* had reached the Gulf Stream current. "Now, laddie, if we should lose our sails this current will take us home. It'd be a slow passage but it would take us home."

* * *

For the rest of that voyage, the bosun let Enig have the reins as it were. He wanted to see what he could do. "You're the boss of the crew now, laddie. You answer to the XO. I'll stand by and watch."

Enig had worked for nearly three months beside Bosun and he had a good idea how he was to preform his duties. Captain Slaugo and the three lieutenants were also watching.

On the second day in the current, Captain Slaugo announced that the *Queen Mary* was now making fourteen knots, steady. "I would imagine there probably is a storm to the south of us and we are reaping the benefits of the high winds," he said.

"Because we are taking a direct route to Glasgow, laddie, we will be sailing a greater distance. But because our speed is faster will cut a few days off the crossing this voyage. You do understand, laddie, that the shortest distance on a sphere is not a straight line?"

"Yes, a curved line is shorter."

"Just checking," Bosun said.

"I'm surprised we haven't seen any icebergs this crossing, Bosun."

"Maybe they melted in the warmer water, or I suppose if they enter the Gulf Stream they might have been taken north of Scotland."

They had encountered several whales that were returning from their summer feeding grounds. And one close encounter with a Great Gray Whale.

The *Queen Mary* arrived at Port Glasgow Navy Base on October 15th and shaved three days off the crossing by using the Gulf Stream current.

"Okay, laddie, it's up to you to get these trees off the *Queen Mary*. I'll stand by just in case."

They came off as smooth as they were put on. One end at a time. When the last one was resting on the dock, Lieutenant

Cohurn said, "Bosun and Seaman McFarney, you are to report the captain's cabin at once."

"What do you suppose this is about, Bosun?"

"I don't rightly know."

"Bosun MacCangus and Seaman McFarney reporting as ordered, Sir."

"At ease, gentlemen. I have your discharge papers, Mr. MacCangus. You'll need to sign them. I wish I could convince you to stay on."

"Thank you, Sir, but I'd have to explain to me wife. And I have the fear, Sir, of doing that."

"You have been a good bosun mate, Mr. MacCangus. And now, Mr. McFarney, on the strong recommendation from Mr. MacCangus, I am promoting you to Bosun mate, to start immediately. Everyone on board ship has been watching you and before I made my discission I talked with my officers and they all agreed. Congratulations, Bosun McFarney.

"As soon as you have the ship completely secure, you have earned two days off. Be back here by 1100 hours on the 17th. Dismissed."

"Thank you, Captain Slaugo."

"And me thanks you, Captain. It was a pleasure serving under you."

"Enjoy your retirement, Mr. MacCangus."

They left the captain's cabin and MacCangus asked, "How about one more pint, laddie?"

"I would, Bosun, but I have to make sure the *Queen Mary* is secured properly."

"That's a good lad. That's what I hoped you'd say. And stop calling me Bosun. You are the bosun now."

"Okay, Fraser," and they shook hands and said goodbye.

Enig walked around the ship and found everything satisfactory and he left the base and he was able to hitch a ride to Greenock on a freight wagon.

CHAPTER 4

The wagon driver dropped Enig off at the mouth of his folks' driveway. Ennis and the entire town knew the *Queen Mary* had returned and Ennis was now at the McFarney house.

When Enig arrived home, Innis was there visiting his folks and she was helping Hilda clean the kitchen after supper. He didn't even knock on the door—instead he just walked in. Innis saw him first and she shouted, "Enig!" and jumped into his arms. Hilda turned around to look and his dad came out of the bedroom.

It was a more joyous reunion than he thought it would be. Hilda and Innis were in tears. Eachann was smiling proudly. "We heard the Queen Mary was back," his dad said.

"How long are you home for, son?" his mother asked.

"I have to report back on the 17th at 1800 hours." When his mom looked confused he said, "6 p.m., Mom."

Then he told them about his promotion while Innis and Hilda were warming up supper leftovers.

"You mean after almost four months you were promoted to Bosun mate? Unbelievable," his dad said. "They had to see something in you, son."

They all wanted to hear all about his travels and his time at sea and the places he had visited. "Did you see any rough weather or seas, son?" his dad asked.

"Off the coast of Cape Hastteras, North Carolina, we ran into some terrible rough water. But the North Atlantic is never calm. At least that is what the others were saying, and we surely didn't see any calm water."

Enig wanted to hear all about the boat building business. "I had to hire three more men. The orders are coming in that fast."

The sun had set two hours ago and Enig thought he had better walk Innis home. "Perhaps I should walk you home now Innis."

Everyone was silent for a few uncomfortable moments. Finally Innis said, "I don't live at home anymore, Enig."

"What happened?" The obvious question.

"Two months ago my father wanted me to marry a well-to-do relative of his. I said no, that you and I would be married after you finish your military duty. He said that I would marry whomever he decided I should marry. I said not hardly and we got into an awful argument. The next morning I packed my things and came here to talk with your mom and dad. I'm not going back to my dad's house. Never."

Eachann said in the old Scottish Burr, "Dinnae marry fur money" (Don't marry for money; you can borrow it cheaper.)

"She has taken over Blair's room and she is welcomed to stay as long as she wants. It is really nice having a daughter in the house again."

Eachann and Hilda finally went to bed and Enig and Innis stayed up until midnight talking. Innis could hear the enthusiasm in Enig's voice as he told her about sailing and visiting different ports and countries. And she was worried he might decide to stay in the navy.

But her fears were for nothing, as the next morning at breakfast Enig said, "I'll be glad when I can get back in the shop with you, Dad."

That day Enig and Innis spent much of their time walking the trails in the hills that overlooked Greenock. Once they were on top there was a warm breeze blowing in from the ocean from the warm Gulf stream.

For supper that evening, Enig took them out to the Scotsman Hotel Restaurant.

That night as Eachann and Hilda were preparing for bed, he said, "Hilda, our son has become a man. This short time in the navy has been good for him."

"I can see the difference, too, Eachann, as does Innis."

While Hilda and Innis were doing some housework and baking the next day, Enig walked over to the boat shop to see what his dad was working on now.

He pitched in and helped until it was time for lunch. In the afternoon, he and Innis went for a walk along the waterfront.

* * *

At exactly 1800 hours, Enig was back aboard the *Queen Mary* and reported to XO Leslie David.

"Welcome back, Bosun."

"Thank you, Sir."

"We are loaded with supplies and will be leaving in the morning with the outgoing tide at 0700 hours. Have your crew ready to set rigging and sails at 0530 hours."

"Yes, Sir."

"Dismissed. And congratulations with your promotion."

The crew were all aboard and he notified them to turn to on deck at 0530 hours.

Two days later after they left the Gulf Stream current, the air temperature dropped noticeably and every morning until they turned southerly there would be a thin film of ice on the decks and rigging.

Enig and Lieutenant Hew McFee, who was in charge of the helm and helmsmen, became quite good friends. Hew was twelve years older than Enig and the *Queen Mary* was the only ship he had sailed on. He had had chances to transfer but he liked the captain, the crew and the *Queen's* sea route. Plus he was a native of Port Glasgow. And he was quite familiar with McFarney boat building shop.

"How much time do you have in the Navy, Lieutenant?"

"I started out as a deckhand when I was eighteen and I worked my way up to lieutenant seven years ago. I turned thirty last summer.

"In two years, I intend to leave the Navy and captain my own merchant ship. Maybe you might consider being my bosun mate. Think about it."

"Nah, I don't think so, Lieutenant. But thank you for asking. Eventually I'll take over my father's boat building business."

Sometimes instead of having a pint or two with the deckhands, Enig would have supper and a pint with Lieutenant McFee. With the lieutenant's company, Enig was not so apt to drink more than two pints, as he would with the crew. He kept his wits about him and no hangovers.

When the *Queen Mary* returned to Great Britain, they didn't always return to Port Glasgow. They hit Liverpool, Tilsbury and New Castle. And every return trip they would bring back two, one-hundred-foot mast stocks.

Some mornings the crew would return from a shore liberty with stories about trouble the colonies were having living under British rule.

When they did return to Greenock, the turnaround was quick and Enig was not able to go home and visit his folks and Innis. These times Captain Slaugo had important dispatches to leave with Admiral Gibbson, and they would be on their way again after picking up supplies.

As the bosun mate, Enig was busy enough so he had very little time to think about home. And quite often he would meet with Lieutenant McFee and they would talk about life beyond the navy.

There was one thing for sure, though. He was looking forward to the end of his enlistment so he could get on with his life.

* * *

The *Queen Mary* was making her return voyage back to Port Glasgow and this would be Enig's last voyage on her. Two days before arriving he was called to Captain Slaugo's quarters. "Come in, Bosun, and have a seat. We are only two days out from Port Glasgow and your enlistment was up three days ago. For someone so young and with so little time at sea you have done a remarkable job. And I would like you to think about re-enlisting for another three years or maybe make the Navy your career."

"Thank you, Sir, but my mind is made up. My father needs my help in the business. I have enjoyed my time aboard the *Queen Mary* and I certainly have learned much. But I must return to Greenock and building boats."

"I understand. I had to try."

Once the *Queen Mary* was secured, Enig already had his duffle bag packed; he said goodbye to the crew and officers and he met Hew McFee at the gangway. "Going ashore, Mr. McFarney?"

"Yes, and you?"

"Going home. Good luck to you, Enig. If your boat building business fails and you need work I will hire you in a minute to sail as my bosun. That's as soon as I can get my own ship."

"What will you name it, Hew?"

"The *Venture*."

"That sounds like a good name. I'll watch for it. May you always follow calm waters. It was a pleasure serving with you, Lieutenant," and Enig saluted one last time. Hew returned the salute.

CHAPTER 5

"Have you had enough of sailing, son?" Eachann asked.

"Yes, but I'm glad I did it. I saw a lot of the world, made some good friends and I certainly learned a lot.

"But now it's time to go back to work."

His father was happy to hear that.

"It's been two years since I was here last. You have expanded, Dad."

"We now employ six men and we have been building six boats a year. Two went to Le Harve, France, two to London and one to Liverpool. The others to local fishermen."

Enig and Innis were married two weeks later and for now they lived with his folks. Hilda and Innis were good company for each other.

Eachann saw immediately how his son was more able to handle the other workers and supervise now. The navy had trained him well. *Probably better than I could have.*

Work was being done faster now and the quality of the boats had improved.

Eachann was now assured that he would be leaving the business in good hands when his time came to leave. His only regret being he wished his other son and daughter, Fergus and Blair, had not left the family and Scotland.

* * *

Life was going good for Enig. He had enjoyed his time at

sea but he was happier working in the boat shop and he adored his wife, Innis. And she had a baby boy in the spring of 1758 and they named him Fergus. When his father asked, "Why Fergus, son?"

"I miss my brother, Dad." That's all that was said.

Eachann enjoyed his grandson, even at an early age. Two years later Innis gave birth to a daughter they named Blair, after Enig's sister that he knew he would never see again.

The boat building business had enlarged with more orders to fill and a bigger shop was built; now the company had twenty men working, besides Eachann and Enig.

Not long after Blair was born, Eachann had a heart attack at work one day and died in the shop.

Hilda had tried to get him to slow down now that Enig was back in the shop and doing most of the supervising, but it wasn't Eachann's nature to sit back and let someone else do his work and run the company.

But work in the shop continued. And he had to hire more help.

Ten months after Eachann died, his mother, Hilda, also died. She had fallen down and broken her leg. It was a bad break and the local doctor had set it and it was in a cast, but during the night she passed. The only explanation the doctor had was that some fat must have gotten in her bloodstream and traveled to the brain causing a stroke.

As grief stricken as they were, work had to continue in the shop.

One day Hew McFee walked into the shop. Enig recognized him at once. "Hello, Hew. What are you doing here?"

"Hello, Enig. I have my own ship now, the *Venture,* and she needs some mast work. I remember how you managed the center mast on the *Queen Mary* and I'm hoping you can do the same for me."

"Where is the *Venture* now, Hew?"

"Tied up at the Greenock docks. The crews are unloading her now."

"Let's go look at her," Enig said.

"Lain, you have the shop. I'm going with the Captain, right?"

"Yes."

"I'm going with Captain McFee to look at his ship that needs repairs."

On the walk to the docks, Hew said, "You have done well Enig."

"Thank you. Both my folks passed not long ago and the company is mine now."

"How many men do you employ?"

"Right now, twenty-two men and my wife, Innis, does all the bookwork and accounting. We also have two children."

Enig followed Hew onboard the *Venture,* and Hew said, "We ran into some heavy winds south of Iceland and the center mast cracked. Not bad, but it needs repair."

Enig walked around the deck looking at the mast.

"What do you think, Enig?"

"I'm thinking we can repair this like we did the mast on the *Queen Mary.* If we cut this mast above the crack and then remove the bottom piece, we should be able to splice in another bottom piece. The same way we did on the *Queen Mary."*

"Where would you get the bottom half?"

"I have one behind my shop that'll work. Is this a rush job, Hew?"

"Can you have it done in a week?"

"I can't see any problem."

"When can you get started?"

"You have your men take down the sails and rigging today. Tomorrow morning me and a crew will start taking the mast down."

"Could I use a couple of your men, if I need extra help?"

"Sure you can. As many as you need."

* * *

Enig left his foreman in charge of the shop and he took six men with him to the *Venture*. Capt. McFee's men were just finishing dismantling the last of the rigging.

Before leaving the shop, he had started soaking enough rope to bind the splice like he had on the *Queen Mary*. By noon they were ready to cut the mast above the crack. They waited until after lunch.

Afterwards the top piece was laid on blocking on the main deck and then they began removing the bottom piece. By the end of the day, they had both sections laying on the blocking on the main deck.

After looking both sections over closely, "Captain, come here would you."

"What is it, Enig?"

"I think I can repair the mast and still use the same two pieces. If I cut the splice in both sections the same as we did on the *Queen Mary,* I can eliminate the crack completely and the repair won't take us as long."

"Whatever you think, Enig. I trust your judgement."

While the men were eating lunch, Enig walked back to the shop to check. "How is everything going, Lain?"

"Just fine; how's your project coming?"

"We may finish up sooner than we originally thought."

While the men ate lunch, Enig spent his time checking and rechecking both sections of the mast, to be sure he made the correct cuts.

It took as much time to bore four holes through the splice for the bolts, as it did to make the cuts for the splice. Four days after they started the repair, Hew McFee came to inspect the work. "It all looks good, Enig. What did you use on the rope?"

"Pine tar mixed with a little coal oil to thin it. The oil will penetrate the rope fiber and preserve it from the weather."

"Enig, I would pay you double wages if you'd be bosun mate onboard The Venture."

"Can't do it, Hew. I have a business now and a family."

"I had to ask."

"How much for the repair?"

"Thirty pounds."

"Where to now, Hew?"

"We'll load up here with hand tools and farm implements. Then in Liverpool we load woven cloth, canvas, tea and mercantile goods.

"When we return, our holds will usually be full of sawn lumber and, like the *Queen Mary*, we'll load two pine tree masts in Belfast. We're usually loaded heavier on the return trip.

"I must get back aboard, Enig. It was good talking with you again and thank you for dropping your work in the shop to make my repairs."

"Have a good voyage, Captain. Anytime you pull into Greenock, let me know and we'll have us a pint."

Back in the shop Enig asked his foreman, Lain Frazier, "How far behind schedule are we?"

"Maybe two days. No more than that."

There were orders waiting and Enig paid his men double to work the weekend. Come Monday morning they were a day ahead of schedule.

* * *

A year had passed since Capt. McFee and the *Venture* had pulled into Greenock, and on a warm July day Enig noticed sails coming up the Strait of Clyde. It was still too far away to recognize. He was hoping it would be the *Venture*.

He opened the shop doors and he and the men went to work. Just before noon he heard a familiar voice and he looked up to find Hew McFee walking towards him.

"I saw a ship coming in the strait and I wondered if it would be the *Venture*. It's lunch time, what say we walk over to my house for lunch. I'd like to introduce you to my wife, Innis.

"Lain, I may be a little late getting back. Carry on, men."

"How did the mast stand up in the high winds and seas?"

"I actually think it is better than before the crack. It sure is stronger. If I have any more mast trouble, I know where to come."

"Innis, this is Captain McFee. Captain, my wife, Innis. And our son, Fergus, and daughter, Blair."

"A pleasure to meet you, Captain McFee."

"Please, it's Hew."

"Are you keeping busy, Hew?" Enig asked.

"Certainly, we seldom get to spend more than two days in a port. Going west to the new world we're loaded with anything from food to furniture, tools and farm animals. On the return trip we're loaded down with lumber, tobacco, bails of cotton and usually two pine tree masts on deck. It's a good business to be in."

"What about the rumors we would hear, are there still such talkings?"

"Yes, but more subtle now. I don't hear things direct, only from my men. The colonists don't like talking in front of me, probably because I captain a ship."

Jokingly, Enig said, "How would you like to move to the new world, Innis?"

"Okay, I'll go with you anywhere you want," she replied.

This certainly surprised him. As well as surprising Hew.

They talked and drank tea for an hour, and Hew said, "I must get back to my ship. Nice meeting you, Mrs. McFarney."

"How long will you be in Greenock?"

"Until the tide goes out about noon tomorrow. We're loading several crates of hand forged tools from the foundry. Maybe you could meet me later this evening for a pint at the waterfront tavern?"

Before answering he looked at Innis first and she said, "Go ahead."

After eating lunch, Hew went back to the ship and Enig back to his shop.

As they were eating supper, Innis asked, "Enig, do you miss sailing?"

"I enjoyed my time in the Navy and I enjoyed visiting foreign ports and countries, but I have no desire to go back." That's what she wanted to hear.

Hew McFee was already at the tavern when Enig arrived early; Hew bought him a pint. "Come, let's sit at the corner table out of the way."

"Hew, let me ask you outright."

"Go ahead."

"Is the *Venture* profitable?"

"Aye, it sure is. I get paid both ways crossing the Atlantic and from port to port, also. A few more years I'm thinking about buying me a bigger ship.

"To do that I might have to sell me investment I bought in Belfast, to come up with enough money."

"What did you buy into Hew?"

"I purchased a tract of land. A grant actually, a half mile square and it sits right on the coast up the bay a short distance from Belfast."

Enig took a drink of beer and then said, "Hew, before you sell that grant would you give me the opportunity first to purchase it?"

"Surely, but what would you want with a grant the size of this one on the opposite side of the Atlantic?" Then he added, "Unless you are planning on moving?"

"I have been toying with the idea, that's all."

"What about your family?"

"There might be some opposition at first from Innis, but I think she would go along with the idea."

"Do you really have that kind of money, Enig?"

"That depends on how much you would have to have."

"250 pounds and not a shilling less."

"I could come up with it."

"Okay, Enig, when my plans start coming together for a new ship, we'll have us a deal," and they shook hands on it and toasted a pint to clinch the deal.

"Let me ask you this, Enig. You have a valuable business here, would you really pack up and move?"

"Well, I'm getting tired of England's domination over us, over Scotland."

"But England rules over the new world also."

"I understand that, but at the same time they are farther away from England and maybe someday they'll break free."

Enig finished his pint and said, "It's time I am on my way home. Every time you're in Greenock, stop by the shop, unless I see the *Venture* coming in. It sure has been good talking with you, Hew."

* * *

It was 10:30 when Enig arrived home and the sun was just beginning to set.

"Did you and Captain McFee have a lot to talk about?" Innis asked.

"We talked mostly about ships and sailing, and I made a promise to Hew to purchase a half mile square grant from him. He is wanting to purchase a bigger ship and when he does, he is going to be needing some money."

"How much is this land going to cost us?"

"250 pounds."

"250 pounds! Have you gone out of your head, Enig? And where is this grant?" she asked.

"In the new world, Innis. Near Belfast, Maine."

"You have gone out of your head." She reverted to her grandad's old Scottish dialect. "Ah dinnae ken. Yer oat yer face or yer off ye rheid."

"I'm not drunk, Innis, and I'm not out of my head. No

money has changed hands yet. I only gave him my promise to buy the land when he needs the money to buy his ship.

"And maybe someday you, Fergus and Blair would find it exciting starting life over in the Americas. You are as fed up with England's domination over us all, as I am."

"This is true." Then she added, "Before we go sailing off for the Americas, I surely hope to wait until Fergus and Blair are a little older."

He relaxed then and fell asleep knowing he was over the biggest hurdle. He was even smiling.

CHAPTER 6

Two years had passed since that summer Hew and Enig agreed on the sale and purchase of Hew's grant near Belfast, Maine. Enig and Innis only talked about it when the two children were not around. They didn't want them telling their friends and the entire town knowing.

Early in July of 1764, the *Venture* pulled into Greenock and tied up and while the cargo was being offloaded, Hew went to see his friend at the boat shop.

"Enig, can we talk in your office?"

"Lain, I'll be busy for a while. You have the shop."

Enig closed the office door. "You have added on to the shop since I was here last. How many men do you employ now?"

"Thirty, plus my wife comes in two days a week to do the books."

"We leave here tomorrow evening with the tide and we'll be empty this time. I am to pick up my new ship at Rosyth, ten miles up the bay from Edinburgh.

"We'll be able to carry almost twice the cargo. It's two hundred and fifty feet long. And she'll be full rigged with bigger and more sails. I can't wait to try her out on the Atlantic."

"With more sail area, I suppose the speed will increase also?" Enig asked.

"If my calculations are correct, we should be able to shorten each trip by two days. That'll be quite an improvement."

"And I suppose you need your money now?"

"Yes."

"I'll have to go to the bank. I don't have that much here."

"That'll be okay. We have to finalize the transaction at the solicitor's office which is next door," Hew said.

"How long will we be, Hew?"

"It shouldn't take us more than an hour. I have had Mr. Graham already prepare the necessary documents."

"Lain, you have the shop. I'll be gone for an hour or so."

"Okay, boss."

At the Bank of England, the clerk asked, "How do you want this?"

"Hew?"

Hew said, "A bank draft will be good. My name is Captain Hew McFee."

"Come in, gentlemen, I have been expecting you. Sit down please. Tea?"

"Yes," they both replied.

"This document, Mr. McFarney, is a description of your property," Mr. Graham said.

"There is a cement corner post at each of the four corners, Enig. The first one, travel up the bay from Belfast approximately one half mile from the Bank of England on Main Street. This document also gives you the coordinates to find the two back corner posts."

"This document, Mr. McFarney, is the transfer of title and ownership."

Enig reviewed this document and then said, "There is one change I would like, Mr. Graham. I will need my wife's name included. Innis McFarney."

"I'll have to have my assistant rewrite this page. It'll be a few minutes."

"While Aria is writing a new page with Innis added, are there any questions, Mr. McFarney?"

"What will become of this new deed?"

"I will file a copy in Greenock's town hall and I will forward another copy with Captain McFee to be filed at the town office in Belfast.

"So as soon as we both sign these documents and I give Hew the money, the property will become mine and my wife's?"

"Yes. Do you have the money?"

"I do. A bank draft made out to Captain Hew McFee."

Aria wasn't long making the change and she handed the document to Enig to peruse. "This is good," he said.

"Good, now if I could have both of your signatures, Aria and I will also sign as witnesses."

Mr. Graham blew the ink dry and he said, "Now, Mr. McFarney, if you would pay the captain, we'll be finished here.

"Aria, we will be needing two copies of these documents, before the afternoon is out."

"Yes, Mr. Graham."

"You gentlemen do not have to wait around here while Aria is making the copies. I'll have a messenger deliver the document to you. You'll be on the *Venture,* Captain?"

"Yes."

"And you'll be in your shop, Mr. McFarney?"

"Yes."

"Thank you for your business, gentlemen, and good luck to you both."

"What will you call the new ship, Hew?"

"The same name, the *Venture*. I kinda like it."

"I'll be looking forward to seeing your new ship in Greenock."

"Well, I'll have to bring her here to pick up more cargo for Halifax. Probably by the middle of August."

* * *

At 4 o'clock that afternoon a messenger delivered the documents to Enig. There was no need to explain to his crew about the purchase.

After Fergus and Blair had gone to bed, Enig showed Innis the documents. "This land is ours now, sweetheart."

"I see you included my name on the deed."

"Yes, why wouldn't I?"

* * *

Now that he was a large landowner in a faraway country, a lot of his spare time was spent thinking of the possibility of moving his family. But on the flip side, he and his family were very comfortable here in Greenock and he had plenty of money. This flip side of his thinking was telling him he would be a fool for giving it all up. He could hear his dad speaking to him from his grave. *Yer aff yer heid* (Are you a bit daft.) Maybe he was, but what an adventure it would be.

* * *

Fergus was now six years old and he would help his dad to clean the shop on Saturday. Enig would watch him and he was happy to see him with such early work ethics and interests with boats.

There were times when he would go out on the boat with his dad fishing, for the family. Enig especially enjoyed these times with his son and if he was to be honest, he actually missed the sea.

One day while he and his son were out fishing an idea began to build in his mind. He would rebuild this boat and sell it, and build another for him. A little bigger and with new improvements the shop had developed.

* * *

A year after Capt. Hew McFee had bought his new ship, Enig saw the tall sails coming into the bay at Greenock. When the *Venture* was tied up and secured, Enig walked down to the docks. Hew was just coming down the gangway. "She's a beauty, Hew. How does she lay in rough waters?"

"Like a slender woman on silk sheets.

"I have to see the harbor master. Go aboard and look around. I won't be long."

The crew were busy unloading crates of cargo and he tried to stay out of their way. It was a sleek, sharp looking ship. He had just finished touring the ship when Hew walked up the gangway.

"She's a sharp looking ship, Hew. How much time can she cut off crossing the Atlantic?"

"Only a day and a half. I thought it would be more. But then again we're loaded heavier, too."

"I noticed two additional cabins on the top next to your quarters."

"We can carry up to six passengers, also. We've carried some pretty important people at times."

"It must be nice, Hew. I must get back to the shop."

Hew walked with Enig down the gangway and asked, "Any plans about moving to Belfast?"

"Yes, but my daughter is only five. I'll wait until she's a little older. It will happen, though, and when it does I hope we can make the trip with you."

"You can count on it, Enig."

"Have a good voyage," and they shook hands.

Back at the shop he went to work helping to finish up another boat. The customer was coming at 5 o'clock that afternoon and Enig wanted it in the water.

During lunch all he could think about was the *Venture* and sailing. Somehow the sea had gotten ahold of him and kept trying to call him back. Then he started thinking about starting life over in Belfast, Maine. What an adventure that would be. Especially for Fergus and Blair.

He finished his lunch and tried to put thoughts of the sea and Belfast out of is mind.

CHAPTER 7

Another five years passed and the McFarney boat building business had increased to the point where he was beginning to turn away customers. And the McFarney reputation for building fine fishing boats had surpassed any builder in the commonwealth. He was making good money and he paid his employees good wages.

Enig and Innis had often talked about moving to Belfast ever since she saw the *Venture* in Greenock one day. But she still insisted that Blair be older. That year Blair would turn ten and Fergus, twelve.

Then one night while lying in bed, Innis said, "Okay, we make the move this year, Enig."

The *Venture* was tied up at the docks in the morning. Even before breakfast; Enig rushed down to talk with Hew.

"We can't do it this trip, Hew, but the next time you're in Greenock. We need the time to sell the business and the house and pack up. I'll want to take my fishing boat and we'll have everything we'll be taking with us stored in that. What will it cost to take my boat?"

"That would go on deck on a jig and be secured. I've shipped other boats before. For the boat, forty pounds."

"Okay, and my family? There are four of us."

"Oh, maybe thirty pounds each. I could sharpen my pencil some if Innis would work in the galley helping the cook and you could help out on deck. But we can discuss this once you're onboard. We're leaving with the tide today and plan to be back in April. Will that be enough time for you?"

"We'll make it happen."

At the supper table that night, Enig told his family, "I have something to say to my family." Innis knew what was coming. "I talked with Captain McFee this morning, and in April we all will board his ship, the *Venture*, for the American Colonies, Belfast, Maine. The *Venture* is a new ship and there are accommodations for six passengers. To cut cost, Hew said you could help out in the galley cooking and I on deck."

"What about me?" Fergus said, "I'm big enough to work."

"Yes you are, son, and maybe the captain will have a job for you.

"From today until we leave, I will have to find someone to buy the business and this house."

"How long will we be gone, Daddy?" Blair asked.

"Belfast, sweetheart, will be our new home.

"There will be details to work out and we will work everything out."

Later that night Enig was sitting alone and thinking that his announcement went better than he had supposed it would. No one objected.

* * *

First thing Monday morning, before work started at the shop, Enig made the announcement to the men and he assured them that he would have it written into the sales agreement that the new owner keep all of the crew.

Innis had put an advertisement in the newspaper that the house and boat business were for sale. Two days later the shop foreman said he wanted to buy the house. They agreed on a price and that Enig and family could live there until they left.

In the middle of March, two businessmen arrived at the boat shop from Glasgow and they were certainly interested in buying the business, the sale to be effective on April 1st, and they had no reservations about keeping the same workforce. "It would be foolish to bring in new people," one of the new owners said.

The money from the sale of the house was more than enough to pay for passage on the *Venture* and the sale of the boat building business netted them another sixteen hundred pounds and they had seven hundred pounds in the bank.

"This will be enough, Innis, to build us a house and to start another boat building business."

That night as they lay in each other's arms Enig said, "You know, wife, I think we are supposed to make this journey to the new world. Everything has gone so smoothly. It's like some *thing*—some *force*—is helping us.

"The more I think on it, husband, the more excited I become. And like you, I also think there is something guiding us. I have always believed that life is not just a random walk," Innis said.

* * *

Enig went through all of his papers; leaving what should stay with the shop and taking others. He especially wanted to take some of the designs, particularly the blueprints for the forming jigs. The jigs themselves would stay but he wanted the design blueprints.

On April 1st, the *Venture* came in with the morning tide and tied at Greenock. The McFarneys were eating breakfast when Innis saw the tall sails go past. "The *Venture* is sailing past the house, Enig."

Enig went first to the shop to open up. "The *Venture* is in, Lain. I'm going over to talk with Captain McFee. You have the shop."

Hew was in his quarters when Enig arrived. "Come in, Enig. Are you ready to leave?"

"Yes. The house and the shop have been sold. All we need to do is load our personal belongings in my fishing boat."

"Good, tomorrow I have cargo for Liverpool and load cargo back for Halifax and the colonies. Then back here on the 18th to load tools from the foundry. Once that is loaded I can load your boat on the eve of the 19th and leave on the 20th with the morning outgoing tide.

"I told you earlier, the passage would be 30 pounds each. I can work out a deal for you. I would like you to sail as bosun mate for me until we arrive in Belfast. My regular man slipped on the icy deck and broke his leg. He should be well enough to make the next voyage. But I need me a bosun for this trip. On the return trip we'll have to make do with my second mate filling in. Your passage, then, will be no charge. I have also talked with our cook and he would like some help in the galley. So your wife's passage will also be free. That leaves your two children—at 30 pounds each, that is sixty pounds, plus your fishing boat at forty pounds. A total of one hundred pounds."

"When do you need your money, Hew?"

"The day you come aboard with your family."

"This is a dream come true. I must leave now, Hew. The sale of the shop closes at noon today."

"I'll see you on the 18th, Enig."

Enig had plenty of time, so he stopped at a café for a cup of tea. As he sipped his tea he began thinking what he would do once they were in Belfast. *First, I'll have to erect something for a shelter. I have brought plenty of canvas for that. Then build a permanent house. With a root cellar. Dig a well. An outhouse. Find enough food for the winter. And once the house is closed in to the weather, I'll have to make furniture.* That last thought gave him an idea.

He had another cup of tea and then he went to Solicitor Graham's office. The two buyers were already there and he was early.

"Mr. Dunn, Mr. Brodie," Enig said.

Mr. Graham handed Enig the sales agreement. "Read this

over, Mr. McFarney, before you sign the sales agreement."

He read every line and reread parts of it. He stopped when he came to the last paragraph. "It says here he wants to continue using the McFarney name for the company."

"Yes, the McFarney name has an excellent reputation in the boat building business and we would like to continue using it until we have established our own reputation. And we are prepared to give you in addition to the selling price of 1600 pounds, an additional 500 pounds. The McFarney name is known all over Europe."

"Give me a few minutes. I need to go outside and walk around and think about this."

"Certainly, take all the time you need, Mr. McFarney," Mr. Brodie said.

After Enig had left, Mr. Dunn said, "I hope he'll accept. Without the name we might be buying a pig in a poke, Carl."

"Maybe we should offer him more money," Carl Brodie said.

Enig hated to sell his name, but with that 500 pounds he and Innis could buy some furniture here and have it shipped to Belfast. He took ten minutes to think it over and come back inside.

"I hate to do it, but for an additional 500 pounds, okay."

Mr. Dunn produced 2100 pounds and Enig signed the agreement. Then Dunn and Brodie did also. Three copies— Solicitor Graham was keeping a copy of the agreement on file.

From there they walked with Enig up to the shop and he introduced the two to the crew. "Lain Frazier has been the foreman here for many years and he'll make you a good company man. The crew, everyone of them are good workers."

Enig left and Dunn and Brodie stayed to get acquainted with Lain and the crew. Before going home he walked along the waterfront, thinking about selling the business his dad had worked so hard to make thrive. "I hope I haven't disappointed you, Dad."

He didn't return home until midafternoon and Fergus and Blair were just getting home from school.

"I thought you'd be home before now, Enig," Innis said. "Did the sale go okay?"

"Yes," and he told her about the extra 500 pounds for using the McFarney name.

* * *

The next morning, after Fergus and Blair had left for school Enig said, "I think you and I should walk over to Buchanon's store and purchase some furniture. If Hew doesn't have room for it then I'll ask Mr. Buchanon if he'll ship it to Belfast."

"What are you thinking we should buy?"

"Three beds and mattresses. You have bedding. I can build a table, but we should have chairs."

They found what they wanted and if Captain McFee didn't have room on the *Venture* this trip, he would send it with the *Venture's* next trip.

They started packing clothes and personal items and these would be put in the fishing boat before the 18th. There wasn't that much that they were taking with them.

One night while Enig and Innis were lying in bed, she said, "Sweetheart, are you sure we are doing the right thing. I mean, here we have a good life. Your boat building business is known throughout the Commonwealth and much of Europe. And we have or had 1000 pounds in our savings. I just do not know if we are doing the right thing." Enig could hear her voice cracking trying to hold back from crying.

"Sweetheart, we have sold the house and business and it's a little late to be having second thoughts. We'll be fine."

"How much money total do we have?"

"4100 pounds, that's including the 1000 pounds from the business account."

"Oh my, Enig, that is a lot of money."

"Yes it is and we'll be just fine."

* * *

On the 15th, Enig and Innis loaded everything into the fishing boat and covered everything with a piece of canvas. Then he took it down to the docks and tied it up out of the way. Then he went to the general store and bought a large amount of garden vegetable seed, everything except potato. Those would spoil before he could plant them the following year.

When he had visited the port at Belfast while onboard the *Queen Mary,* he knew there were shops in the village but he had no idea what they would have for supplies. There were wooden framed houses so there had to be a sawmill. There was brick work on some of the shops, so there was a foundry.

He knew they would be starting life all over, but they had one thing in their favor. They had enough money for a new beginning.

Where he and Innis were plagued with worries and concerns, Fergus and Blair were excited and they couldn't wait to set sail upon the Atlantic Ocean.

* * *

The *Venture* pulled into the Greenock docks the next day on the 17th, a day early. "Innis, the *Venture* is in port and I'm going down to talk with Hew."

"Okay."

Hew was walking down the gangway, "Good morning, Enig. Are you ready?"

"Yes, everything has been done and my fishing boat is tied up at the end of the docks."

"Good, we're a day early and if you are ready to go, then we can go a day early on the 19th."

"That'll be okay. I have one question. Innis and I bought three beds and some smaller articles. Would you have room in one of the holds? Everything has been crated."

"I don't think that'll be a problem. We'll have to load that crate before we do your boat. The boat will go on last.

"I have to see the harbormaster now, Enig."

"One more question. When do you want us to board?"

"On the 18th at 1800 hours."

"When do I start as bosun?"

"You'll have things to do until you board on the 18th, so you'll start your duties at 0600 hours on the 19th."

"I really must leave now," he said.

He walked home and told his family when they had to board the *Venture* and that they would be departing a day early on the 19th.

"I'll be glad when we are on our way. Maybe then I can relax. I am so nervous now."

He hugged Innis and said, "Everything will be okay." She laid her head on his shoulder. "I hope so."

Before going to bed, Innis and Enig sat down and talked with Fergus and Blair. Innis was shocked. Neither one had any reservations about leaving here forever and starting a new life in a far away land. They both were actually excited and couldn't wait to be on the ship.

CHAPTER 8

The 18th came and Enig and family walked up the gangway. Captain Hew McFee was on the deck to welcome them aboard. Enig and Fergus were carrying the chest with all of their clothes and personals, and all the money they had. "Welcome aboard, Enig, Innis, Fergus and Blair. Follow me and I'll show you to your quarters. As I said earlier, Enig, you'll have the bosun's quarters and a set of bunks have been added for your children. The cabin is small, but you should be quite comfortable.

"After you unpack, I would like all of you to come to my quarters. We need to talk. I think you know where to find it, Enig."

"Yes, Captain."

The captain left and Enig said, "From here on when you address him, it is always Captain. You do not call the captain by his given name."

There wasn't much unpacking to do. "Let's go see what the captain wants to talk about." Enig also took enough money to pay for their passage.

Enig knocked on his door. "Come in. Sit down, please."

"Captain, I owe you 100 pounds plus how much for the crate you brought onboard?"

"It isn't taking any unwarranted space so maybe 5 pounds. That'll cover the cost of handling."

Enig counted out 105 pounds and gave it to the captain.

"Life on aboard any ship is so much different than what

you are used to. I have to maintain discipline at all times or there will be problems. Whenever you address me, it must be Captain McFee. You all are my friends, but I expect the same level of discipline as I would the crew.

"Enig, you already know what your duties are. Innis, you will work in the galley with Boyd James, chief cook. You'll turn to each morning at 0500 hours.

"Fergus, you're a big strapping lad like your father. There may be times when your father could use your help keeping the decks clean.

"Blair, how old are you?"

"I'll be ten soon."

"You are a pretty young girl. And all the hands on deck also noticed. Females can wreak havoc among men who spend a lot of time at sea. So I do not want you to roam the decks by yourself. Ever, I'm not being harsh or trying to scare you. I'm only trying to prevent trouble before it happens. And to keep you from being hurt.

"If you get bored, Blair, you might be able to help your mother in the galley. Perhaps with dishes."

"Depending on the weather, the crossing will take about three weeks.

"Fergus, once we enter iceberg alley, maybe you could help keep watch on the bow."

"Innis, every morning the AB seaman on duty will wake you at 0430, so you'll be able to turn to in the galley at 0500."

"If anyone has any questions during the voyage, just ask."

* * *

At 0430 the next morning, AB Paul Heming knocked on the McFarney's cabin door. Innis was already up and so, too, was Enig. Both ready to go to work. Fergus and Blair went to the galley and helped to set the long table. Blair liked being a helper but Fergus would rather be on deck helping his dad.

Fergus could hear his dad issuing orders and he went

out on deck to watch. Rigging was being prepared to set the sails. Captain McFee and his chief mate, Rory Douglas, were in the captain's quarters plotting their course. Only his dad was on deck ordering the crew. He was suddenly very proud of his dad. He stayed out of the way watching. He was very interested watching the men preparing to set sails.

Half the crew went in for breakfast while the others continued working.

Blair started bringing breakfast plates to each man. And so far no one had made a rude remark. Innis was watching.

Without any warning Chief Mate Douglas stepped out on the bridge, "Bosun McFarney!" he bellowed.

"Yes, Sir."

"Set the bow spirit and the starboard bow jib and main sails top to bottom. When we are clear the harbor, you know what to do then," the chief mate said.

"Aye aye, Sir."

A strong gust of wind came over the top of the highland behind Greenock and caught the main sails rocking the ship. Innis felt this, as could everyone else. "We're on our way, Blair. There's no looking back now."

"Dad, can I go up to the bow and watch?" Fergus asked.

"Yes, just stay out of everyone's way, son."

The *Venture* was an hour before she cleared the harbor. Then Enig and crew went to work setting all the sails. Fergus watched all of this with fascination. Even on deck looking up through the sails, the *Venture* was an impressive looking ship.

After the sails were all set, Enig stood by his son. "Any regrets, son?"

"No. There is a lot of water out here isn't there, Dad."

Enig chuckled and said, "There sure is. You wait until we have been out here for weeks and no sight of land. You'll begin to wonder if there is any."

"When we get into some rough seas, son, you'll want to be

careful out on deck."

"I will."

"Are you hungry? We kinda missed breakfast."

"I'm okay, Dad."

* * *

To free up a deckhand, Fergus was asked to stand the day watch at the bow for icebergs. "If you see a berg, ring this bell five times and holler out its location; straight ahead, port or starbird," the chief mate said.

"Aye, aye, Chief."

Fergus liked this duty, although he did get hungry at times ... until his mother started making up a lunch for him to take with him.

Innis was doing all the baking now and the crew enjoyed Blair waiting on them. And sometimes small amounts of money would be left on the table for a tip.

Enig was enjoying being a bosun mate again, and the men all liked him.

There were long hours each day for the whole family, but no one was complaining. Enig always enjoyed working. Innis was enjoying cooking for a crew of hungry men, and showed her respect and friendliness. Fergus was enjoying his duty as watchman on the bow. He often would see schools of whales, porpoises, flying fish and sharks in the warmer Gulf Stream current.

They all were tired at the end of each day and the rolling ship would put them all to sleep soon after lying down.

One day after lunch, Enig went to see Captain McFee in his quarters. "Come in, Bosun. What can I do for you?"

"Oh nothing special, I just came up to talk. We'll be arriving in Belfast soon and we haven't had the opportunity to talk much socially."

"No, we haven't. You and your family have adapted very well and easy to sea life. I don't suppose I could talk you and your family to sail with me permanently? The entire crew speaks well of your family."

"Thank you, Hew, but I'm afraid not. We all are set to start a new life.

"How fast will this ship go?"

"We have averaged, this voyage, 16 knots. There were two times for a short time when we were sailing at 18 knots."

"She's a nice ship, Hew."

"A word of advice, Enig, once we are on shore; get your deed properly registered as soon as you can. There is a land agent in the center of town that will take care of it for you."

"I'll do that before we even go out to look at it."

They talked for two hours before Hew had to return to work. As did Enig.

"One more question, Hew. Is there someplace we can store the crate with our bedding?"

"There is a storehouse at the port. I know the harbor master and I'll ask him for you."

"Thank you."

* * *

Eighteen days after Greenock, the *Venture* sailed into the Belfast port. The ship was tied up and the sails brought in and secured. "Welcome to Belfast, Enig, Innis, Fergus and Blair. It was a pleasure having you aboard."

Enig and Fergus carried their chest of clothes and personables to the small terminal building. "Come with me, Enig."

Enig followed him to the harbormaster's office, Stuart Douglas. "Hello, Captain McFee. How was your crossing?"

"It was as smooth as glass."

"Not the North Atlantic."

"No, but it was a good crossing. I want you to meet Enig McFarney. He and his family made the voyage with me and are going to start a new life here. I sold them the property I had up river. He has a crate that he needs to leave undercover until he is ready for it. Can you help him, Stuart?"

"Seeing how he is your friend, certainly I can. That warehouse on the end is empty."

"He'll need a horse and wagon to move it."

"No problem. You unload the crate and I'll have two men store it for you."

"Thank you, Mr. Douglas."

Captain McFee had to talk with the harbormaster, Stuart Douglas, and collect his fee for the goods that would be left there. "Hew, I don't know if I'll get another chance to thank you for everything you have done for us. But I certainly speak for everyone when I say thank you."

"We'll be leaving as soon as the cargo is unloaded here. But we'll stop for cargo for our return trip. I wish you the best and I hope to see you often, Enig. You're a great bosun. Goodbye and good luck."

The fishing boat had already been lowered into the water and tied up.

Two men with a wagon showed up just as McFarney's crate was being unloaded and the boom operator lowered it onto the wagon.

"Did you check and make sure we packed everything, Innis?" Enig asked.

"I'm sure and Blair double checked."

"What now, Daddy?" Blair asked.

"We find a place to stay."

"What about our money, Enig?" Innis asked.

Enig patted his waist and said, "It is all right here in a money belt."

For now their chest was left with the crate in the storehouse, the doors were locked and Enig pocketed the key.

They stopped first at a tavern and asked the owner if he knew where they could find a place to stay.

"If you're not to fussy, I have a flat upstairs. How long will you be needing it?" Ross Maciver asked.

"Three days at least. Until we can set up a temporary shelter on our land up river."

"A half mile up river is it?"

"Yes, we bought it from Captain McFee."

"Aye—and a mighty nice piece of land it is, too. What is your name?"

"Enig McFarney," and he introduced his family.

"You won't be the McFarney that builds fishing boats are you?"

"Yes, we're from Greenock. After we are settled in, we will build another boat building shop here."

"The flat is 2 shillings a day and your meals will be extra."

He showed them upstairs and Innis said, "This will be fine, Mr. Maciver."

All four then went back to the storehouse and carried the chest up to their room.

"What do you say we have an early lunch downstairs then sail the boat up to find our land?"

"I'm hungry," Fergus said.

After eating they climbed aboard the fishing boat. There was a breeze coming off the ocean and they made good time up river. "There," Fergus said, "that's a cement corner post."

"I think you're right. We'll put ashore here and look around."

"Is this land ours, Mommy?" Blair asked.

"Yes it is," Innis said.

A short distance up river from the corner post they came to a slight rise and the land was partially opened. "It looks like this knoll was burned over." There was a small cove and an inlet stream that circled partway around the knoll. The water was deep and Enig said, "This is where we will build."

"Let's unload the boat and we'll cover everything with

canvas. I brought plenty of canvas to make a shelter for us while we build the house."

"This is such a pretty spot, Enig. I can't wait until we can start building our house," Innis said.

After the boat was unloaded and everything was under the canvas, they went exploring. "Look at all the pine trees, Dad," Fergus said.

"Nice aren't they; there's also spruce, cedar and maple."

"How much land is there, Dad?" Fergus asked.

"There's a half mile square block. More than one hundred and sixty acres."

They made a small circle around the knoll and found a narrow deadwater that made up on the stream. "These bushes are high bush cranberries."

"Dad, what's that giant animal up at the other end?" Blair asked all excited.

"It's too big for a deer, elk or caribou. It must be a moose. We have cranberries and meat on the hoof in our own backyard."

Innis could feel his excitement and she started laughing.

"Fergus, I think we'll bring the boat up and in this cove and pull it in far enough so it can't be seen from the river. This will be a good place to store it for now."

While they were doing that, Innis and Blair wandered out back to the base of some high ground. There was a bubbling spring. Enig started hollering for them and they walked back. "Where were you?"

"We walked out back towards the high ground. We found a bubbling spring."

"If you leave the boat here, Daddy, how are we going to get back to town?" Blair asked.

"We walk. It's only a half mile."

"It sure feels good to be able to walk on solid ground. I was beginning to feel cooped up onboard the *Venture*. But still, I did enjoy myself and working. I really felt like part of the team,"

Innis said.

While Enig and Innis brought up the rear, talking, Fergus and Blair ran up ahead exploring. "Fergus, there's a road here."

"Run back and tell Mom and Dad to hurry." Blair ran back.

"Mom, Dad, Fergus and me, we found a road. Come, hurry!" and she ran back where Fergus was.

Enig and Innis looked at each other and Enig said, "A road?"

"Let's go see," Innis said.

"Look," Fergus said, "Someone has cut a road through the forest."

"You three wait right here, I'm going to see where this corner post is." He didn't have far to go. "Innis can you see me?"

"Yes."

"I can't see Fergus. Come halfway between us."

She did. "Our property line is about twenty feet that way. Maybe Capt. McFee had hired a crew to swamp out a road to the property. Let's follow this and see if a loaded wagon could make it through."

There were no big trees. "This looks like an old burn and the spruce and fir trees are just coming back. The soil is dry and sandy."

There were no big stumps and once in a while the road had to swing one way or the other around a rock. "We might have to get us a mule and a wagon."

They eventually came to a graveled road only a stone's throw from town. "This must be a town road."

"I'm going upstairs, Enig, and rest," Innis said.

"I'm going to find a bank."

"Dad, alright if I walk around town?" Fergus asked.

"I want to go too."

"Okay, take your sister."

Enig checked at the post office first and discovered that what passed for a bank was in the same building. He was shown the safe. It stood six feet tall and certainly looked solid and safe. "I want to deposit 3000 pounds in my name, Enig McFarney, and my wife, Innis." He kept the rest to build the house and for food.

From there he walked to the sawmill and talked with one of the owners, a Mr. Camron Hall. Enig introduced himself and said, "Me and my family are building a house and I would like to order some material."

"What will you be needing Mr. McFarney?"

"The walls are going to be 8"x 8". Do you handle anything that rugged?"

"Yes we do."

"Would you have it in pine and dry?"

"I have some pine logs that have been drying. How much will you be needing?"

Enig gave him a material list that he had worked up in the evenings aboard the *Venture*. "This is a big order."

"I have one question, Mr. Hall. Would it be possible for you to deliver to our site?"

"Where are you building?"

"I bought the land from Captain McFee. Apparently he had a road cleared to the property line and our building site is a short distance from there."

"How is the ground on this cleared road?"

"Dry and sandy. Moss covered right now."

"I guess that won't be a problem. I'll have to charge you extra, you understand."

"Certainly. Those items I check marked we'll be needing first. Also, I would like to keep a running account here. I can give you 100 pounds now as a deposit. With a receipt of course."

"Of course. That'll be fine. How soon will you be needing the first delivery?"

"We arrived yesterday on the 10th, today is the 11th, Thursday. We need to erect a temporary shelter, so if you could make the first delivery on Tuesday the 16th, that would be good.

"And then for the 8x8s a week later?"

"There's something I forgot about—the 8x8s, can you plane one side? This will be the interior wall."

"We can do that."

"Is there anything else I can do for you?"

"Is there a blacksmith shop and stables here?"

"Yes, take the road behind the post office, you can't miss it."

"Thank you. What's his name?"

"Craig Randall.

"Thank you, Mr. McFarney; this is the first time a customer has paid up front for lumber. McFarney, that name sounds familiar. Your account says Scotland. Yes, by gorry, McFarney Boat Building Company in Greenock. I have one of your boats. Are you going to start building boats in Belfast, Mr. McFarney?"

"Yes, but we have a lot to do to get settled. Do you saw hardwood? Oak?"

"Yes, we do."

"Good."

* * *

"Excuse me, Smitty, are you Mr. Randall?"

"I be, what can I do for you? You're on foot."

"We only arrived in town yesterday and all I have for transportation is a fishing boat."

"And?"

"I would like to rent me a mule and wagon."

Mr. Randall put his tools down and took his leather apron off and said, "Come with me.

"I made this wagon five years ago. It's strong. Mule is in the barn, come."

"It's a nice looking mule, Mr. Randall."

"Mule is four years old. Strong mule."

"How much would you charge me a day to rent the mule and wagon?"

"I not rent, I sell mule and wagon."

"How much?"

"2 pounds, 6 shillings."

"You throw in the harness."

"Okay."

"I'll come after the mule and wagon tomorrow morning after breakfast and I will have the money for you."

From the stables, Enig stopped at the general store for a keg of nails and a keg of long spikes for the 8x8's. "I'll pick these kegs up tomorrow."

It was almost time for supper but first he told his family what he had been doing.

* * *

After an early breakfast Friday morning, Enig and Innis went to the stables and paid Mr. Randall. Then they stopped at the general store for the two kegs. Then at the tavern to load the chest.

"Before we leave, Enig, we need to buy some food."

Innis bought beans, flour, salt, sugar, tea, salt pork and ham. "This will be a start, Enig."

It was only 10 o'clock when they arrived at the site where they would build the house. "Fergus, rock up a firepit over here and I'll unload the wagon."

"Blair and I will start some beans cooking and store the rest in the shade."

The mule was unharnessed and tied out to graze. Then Enig and Fergus began clearing a place to set up the canvas tarp.

By lunchtime the area was cleared and they sat down to fried salt pork, pan bread and tea.

* * *

By the time all of the first lumber delivery was unloaded Enig and Fergus had dug a hole for a root cellar and had rocked it up with rocks from the shore. They had also dug out a hole near the bubbling spring and had made a crude wooden cold storage box. "There this will keep our food from spoiling."

While the men were working on the root cellar, Innis and Blair took the mule and wagon to town for more stores.

While Enig and Fergus worked on the root cellar, Innis and Blair did the best they could to make their canvas shelter comfortable. They made fir bough beds so they wouldn't have to sleep on the ground and they hung another piece of canvas across the front of the lean-to to block the night breeze.

At low tide they combed the sandy shore digging clams and gathering seaweed.

By the time the next load of lumber arrived, Enig and Fergus had almost finished the root cellar. A day and a half later they had the deck done and while they waited for the 8x8 logs they rocked up under the deck.

Fergus was really enjoying the hard work. It was the first time in his life that his father was treating him like an equal. Like a man. He was only twelve years old but he was big for his age.

Innis noticed the change between father and son and she would often smile.

It took two days for the wagon crew to bring out all of the 8x8s, and Enig and Fergus would have the load in the walls and spiked down before the next load arrived. By the end of the second day, they had the four walls up and another two days to build the two gable ends.

They now had all of the lumber that Enig had ordered, even the boards to close in the roof.

"Enig, this is Sunday. I think we should take this day and rest. You and Fergus are building this house much faster than I would have thought possible."

"That might be a good idea, Innis. We can dig some clams and try fishing."

"Fergus, do you want to fish while the rest of us dig for clams?"

71

"Sure."

"Okay, let's bring the boat out front and I'll push you out and you can fish from that and I'll tie it off onshore so I can pull you back in. Get some bait and I'll bring the boat around."

Fergus dug up a few clams to use as bait. He climbed in and Enig pushed the boat out and said, "Okay drop the anchor there, son."

It was low tide and Enig, Innis and Blair walked upstream a short ways to a sandy flat where Blair had earlier found clams. With three digging, they weren't long before they had a bucket full. And they put some seaweed on top and hiked back.

The tide was coming in now. "Any luck, son?" Innis asked.

"You bet. Before the tide started coming in I caught four nice lobsters. Now I'm catching mackerel."

"How many mackerel do you have?"

"Four."

"That's enough, son, with lobster and clams. I'll pull you in. Lift the anchor." Innis and Blair carried the full bucket back to the lean-to.

"Find some firewood, Blair."

Enig and Fergus cleaned the fish on shore and threw the innards in the water. Their arms were full carrying everything back to camp. The fire was going. "Fergus, you and Blair go get more seaweed. Enough so we can steam everything in seaweed," Innis said.

While they were doing that, Enig put the boat back where it was. It didn't take the two long to bring back two armloads of seaweed.

While the fish, clams and lobster were steaming in the seaweed, Innis asked, "How are we going to heat the house, Enig?"

"Tomorrow, why don't you and Blair take the wagon to town and see what there is at the general store. If Mr. Cummins can order something."

"I can get some more supplies, too."

"That might be a good idea. You might stop at the sawmill and ask Mr. Hall for fifty, eight foot 2x4s."

It took a while to cook all of the seafood but when it was done, it was delicious. "I have never tasted such nice seafood," Innis said.

"I could live on lobster," Blair said. "Except I don't like these spiny things on the shells."

"You know," Fergus said, "All of this food was caught right out our front door. I am beginning to like this America."

* * *

The next day, Monday, Innis and Blair stopped at the general store first. "Good morning Mrs. McFarney, and how is the new house coming?"

"They are setting the roof rafters today. We are in need of a cook stove and a heating stove."

"I have one cook stove. It is out back if you want to look at it. This is porcelain with a hot water heat jacket in back, if you ever get water piped into the house."

"I'll take it, but I need to take back a load of 2x4s today. I'll pay you and come back after it tomorrow, if you can load it in our wagon."

"My son will help me. You'll need some stove pipe, too. I'll send six pieces with you and a roof jack."

"Now what about a heater stove?" Innis asked.

"I have five coming in on the *Venture* from Pennsylvania in two weeks. I'll save one for you and enough stove pipe."

"Would you have a picture I could look at?"

Mr. Cummings reached under the counter and brought out an advertisement. "Here. I have one in my home. It does an awfully good job of heating the whole house. It's called a Franklin Fireplace. Invented by Benjamin Franklin." Mr. Cummins saw the blank look on Innis' face and said, "You do know who Benjamin Franklin is, don't you?"

"I'm afraid not."

"He is a very smart man, an inventor and a powerful statesman."

"Okay, do I pay now for the heater stove or when it comes in?"

"When it comes in."

"Just be sure you save one for us, Mr. Cummins. Now we need to pick up some food supplies."

She got more beans and salt pork, three loaves of bread and five pounds of butter, tea, sugar and salt.

"Everything comes to 15 pounds and seven shillings."

From the general store they went to the sawmill and a crew loaded the 2x4s. "Mrs. McFarney, tell your husband there is 30 pounds left on your account."

"Thank you, Mr. Hall. Good day."

* * *

"I ordered a Franklin Fireplace stove and it will come in on the *Venture* from Pennsylvania in two weeks. We also bought a cook stove which you and Fergus should go in tomorrow morning and help load it in the wagon. Mr. Hall also said there is 30 pounds left on the account."

Blair took care of the food stores while Fergus unloaded the lumber. He unhooked the wagon and took the harness off the mule and staked it out to feed where it could reach water.

Enig and Fergus left early the next morning. The roof rafters were all on. There were enough boards to close in one side but not both.

After the stove was loaded, Enig asked, "Mr. Hall, do you have windows?"

"They're in a building out back. I only have the double hung windows."

"That'll be fine. We'll need eight. Although I don't know if we can take 'em all this trip."

They could only take three with the stove. "Someone will

74

be after the other five tomorrow." Enig paid him and went to see Mr. Hall.

"What can I do for you today, Mr. McFarney?"

"We need another wagonload of twelve inch boards to close the roof in. Probably two loads as I intend to double board the roof. I'll also need some tongue and groove 1x6 boards. And do you have cedar shingles or shakes?"

"Yes both, which do you want?"

"The shakes."

"How many squares?"

"Six for now."

Because of the windows, it was a slow trip back.

* * *

Another week had passed and the roof was double boarded and covered with thick cedar shakes. The windows and doors were made but not yet hung. He would need some nice pine finish boards for the interior doors and to frame the windows and doors.

"What are you going to put on the interior walls, Enig?"

"I'm not going to fool around with lathes and plaster. So I thought pine tongue and groove boards would look nice."

One day as they were finishing the interior walls with pine, "Dad," Blair said. "There's a wagon coming."

Enig went out to see, and Capt. McFee pulled up and stopped. "Hello, Hew," Enig said. When Enig said his name, everyone came out to say hello.

"I like what you have done here. I brought you your Franklin Fireplace from Cummins store. I'll help you carry it inside. It is heavy.

"I like the idea and looks of the square logs. They'll really look nice with a clear finish.

"I'm really surprised you have done so much already."

"There is still a lot of inside work to do, but we're sleeping under a roof now. And sleeping on a bed is so much better than the ground."

"Would you like some tea, Captain?"

"Please, you don't have to call me Captain now. It's Hew. And yes, I would like a cup."

They talked and drank tea for an hour and Hew said, "I must be leaving now. The crew is filling the holds and topside with sawn lumber."

"How's the ship?"

"The *Venture* is a good ship. She should last me for several years."

* * *

By the end of June, the house was complete with a front porch and steps. And the interior woodwork had been varnished. While the varnish dried, they had to sleep outside for two nights because of the fumes.

The next project was to clear the land around the house and back to the spring. The spring was high enough to provide gravity fed water once he had a ditch dug and water pipe laid.

While Enig dug the ditch, Fergus and Blair continued clearing the brush and small trees and burning them. The soil was sandy all the way back to the spring and he had the ditch dug, pipe laid and backfilled in four days.

"Dad what about this rock? It's the only one in the clearing. It looks like a big kidney."

"We leave it for now. Some time we'll see if we can move it."

"It's an odd rock, Dad," Fergus said.

"What do you mean?"

"It's the only rock on the surface in this whole area. It is shaped like a kidney and the color does not match any of the rocks along the shore. It's out of character."

"I have thought about it, and maybe when we have more time we can work on it and come up with some answers."

* * *

With the house complete, with the gravity fed water to the kitchen sink, it was time to build a small barn/shed for the mule. He wanted it big enough to use for a workshop and to store firewood. So back to Hall's lumbermill for more 6x6s, this time. But this time they didn't have to be of such good quality or planed on one side.

By the middle of August, the building was complete. "Now we need firewood, son."

The land behind the spring leveled off and was pretty much flat. And there was an abundance of hardwood trees, rock and white maple, oak, ash and yellow birch and some beechnut.

While the men worked on firewood, Innis and Blair made wagon trips to town to stock up with food for the winter. Mr. Cummins at the store told them about the MacDonald Farm a mile out of town where they could buy fresh vegetables; pick your own.

Innis bought three dozen mason jars for canning. When she and Blair were finished, the root cellar was almost full.

Enig and Fergus worked every day on firewood, averaging about a cord each day; cut, split and piled. The first several days they cut standing dead trees and piled the dry firewood on the porch.

Every Sunday they would have a family day and steam clams, lobster and fish in seaweed. "We never ate this good in Greenock," Fergus said.

Enig and Fergus built a smoker and one day the two went fishing for haddock and cod out in the ocean. Enig showed his son how to sail—how to rig and position the sails, even when going into the wind. They soon had enough fish and Enig said, "Okay, son, take us back."

The wind was coming at them a little east of north. Enig watched as his son repositioned the main sail at an angle to catch the wind and he pulled in the bow spirit sail. They were soon in the bay. "That was good, son."

Not wanting to ram the boat ashore he pulled the main sail in and brought the boat in for a soft approach. "I think we need a wharf, son."

"If you want to start the fire in the smoker, son, I'll start cleaning the fish."

Innis and Blair came down to see how they had done. "That should see us through the winter."

"Enig, I need to go into town tomorrow and see about getting Fergus and Blair in school. And what are you going to do about feed for the mule?"

"I'll have to start cutting grass in the marsh and probably we'll end up buying some oats from farmer MacDonald."

CHAPTER 9

By the middle of September, Enig had all the marsh grass cut and dried and in the barn that he could get to without having to walk in the water. If the need should arise, there were many bushes the mule had already been feeding on and he could bring some in for it. Right now the mule was still feeding on the new grass that had come up in the clearing around the house.

There was just enough room in the root cellar for all of the smoked fish. "When will you build your shop for building boats, Enig?"

"It won't be this year. Maybe next year. We were really up against the wall this year with the house and barn, putting up enough food for winter and firewood.

"Boy, I never worked this hard back home."

"Do you miss back home, Enig?"

"I have good memories of home, but I don't miss it. Life here has been rough but it'll smooth out in a few years."

"I've been too busy, too, to think about back home," Innis said.

Fergus and Blair were both in school and since the school was only a half mile from home, they walked each day. The schoolhouse was actually near the end of the road they used to go to town.

"Enig," Innis said, "Fergus and Blair are in school and we have been too busy and tired to even think about sex."

Enig was grinning and he stood up and took his wife's

hand and said, "Well it's time we did something about that."

* * *

In October the whole family went out into the marsh and picked a bushel of high bush cranberries. "Dad! Dad!" Blair said all excited, "What is that?" and she pointed to a tall lanky animal about one hundred yards away.

"That's no deer, caribou or reindeer. Maybe an elk," Enig said.

Fergus said, "I think that is another moose. I've seen pictures in our science book. But the one in the book had large antlers. This must be a cow moose. They don't have antlers."

"Oh, Enig," Innis said, "There's enough meat standing there to more than see us through the winter."

"I think you're right. But I'll have to wait for cold weather as we'll have to hang it in the barn. There's no more room in the root cellar.

"Before I even plan on shooting a moose, I'll have to get some new powder. My powder is so old it probably wouldn't ignite."

In late November, artic cold blew in and the ground froze and the marsh. A week ago, Enig had decided it was time to shoot a moose. He had new powder and he kept watch in the marsh and the moose was always on the further shore. Now with the marsh solidly frozen, he left the house at daylight and went out to a point of land about halfway up the marsh. This was as close as he was going to get. He didn't have long to wait and the cow moose came out to feed.

He braced himself in a crotch of a cedar tree. He took his time and waited for the moose to turn towards him. He wanted a clear shot at the base of the neck. His chance came and he fired.

Between the recoil of the rifle and the powder smoke he didn't know if he had hit his target or not. He reloaded and then started across, ready in case he missed or the moose got up. But he didn't have to worry. "Hmm, I'm surprised. It's been years since I even fired this." He had bought the rifle new before he went to sea on the *Queen Mary*. It had cost him more money than he earned in a month;the 50 caliber Brown Bess made by the Royal Armouries Company. He was now glad he had decided to buy it.

He hiked home to get Fergus to help him. "We'd better take the mule. You find an axe and some rope and I'll put the harness on the mule."

"Can I go with you, Daddy?" Blair asked.

"Put on some warm clothes and your boots."

The mule was glad to be outside in the crisp air and it was feeling frisky. He had gotten this out of himself by the time he could smell the dead moose. Blair tied him to a tree. "We'll have to roll it on its back. Okay, Blair can you hold a front leg to steady it? Fergus, hold both rear legs and spread them as much as you can."

He cut the hide up to the ribs. "This hide is thick and tough. Maybe we'll be able to use it for something."

Watching her dad pull the stomach contents out didn't bother Blair. She found it interesting. When he had finished, both arms were covered with blood up to his elbows.

"Okay, Fergus, see if you can get the mule to back up enough so I can tie the rope around the neck."

If there had been a little snow the mule would have been able to drag the moose easier. There were times when Enig would have to help pull. But they eventually made it back. "Blair go in and bring out your mother's big dishpan for the heart and liver."

They pulled the moose up off the ground with block tackle suspended from a heavy pine tree limb. The hide came off easy. Then he pulled the heart and liver out and Blair took it into the house.

"What are we going to do with the hide, Dad?" Fergus asked.

"Let's nail it to the barn wall on the outside and let it dry."

When they had the hide nailed up, they quartered the moose and hung everything in the barn. Later after the meat had frozen, Enig would find a place to hang it in the root cellar.

For supper that night, they had heart, liver and onions with hot biscuits.

Everyone thought the meat was delicious. "It isn't like beef at all and there's so much of it," Innis said.

Later that evening as they were sitting around the fireplace, Enig said, "You know I thought I might be able to do some fishing on the ocean this winter but I don't think so now. The temperature is too cold and water spray would freeze on to the boat and sails and that wouldn't be good.

"Instead, I think I'll work on plans for a boat building shop. I also need to draw plans for a wharf out front."

That weekend Enig and Fergus brought the fishing boat out of the water and after removing the master, they covered it with the canvas canopy. "I really thought we'd be able to fish this winter."

Early in December, the temperature near zero degrees and none of the McFarneys had ever seen temperatures this cold. "Enig, in Scotland the temperature seldom dropped below freezing. We are farther south here and I naturally thought it would be warmer."

"The ocean current, the Gulf Stream, brought warm air up from the equator. The Gulf Stream doesn't even come close to the Maine coast."

"I hope we have enough firewood," Innis said. "I hate to make the kids walk to school when it is so cold."

"They'll have to have good boots and warm clothes."

In her spare time, she began knitting mittens and sweaters for the family. Fergus and Blair came first.

Some nights Enig tied a wool blanket on the mule to help it keep warm. If he had more farm animals that would help to keep the barn warmer and that meant more time and work, which he couldn't afford right now.

The cold spell let up a week before Christmas and Innis took the mule and wagon into town for supplies. She bought extra flour, sugar, salt, eggs and two ten gallon sealed milk cans. She timed her trip so she could pick the kids up after school, so they wouldn't have to walk.

Just as they started moving, Blair said, "What is that noise, Mom?"

She had wanted to wait until they were home, but that wasn't going to happen now. "Look in the top wooden crate. Be careful, don't fall off the wagon."

"The puppy is for you, Fergus, and the kitten is yours, Blair."

Even back in Greenock the two had never had any pets. And Innis promised herself that once they were settled she would see that they did.

Enig wasn't at all upset. "How old are they, Innis?"

"The kitten is eight weeks and the puppy is—I think he said they both are eight weeks."

"You two will have to find a name for them now."

"Is the kitten a boy or girl Mom?" Blair asked.

"I think a boy, but I can't tell by looking."

They both put the kitten and puppy inside their shirts where it was warm. By the time they were home the kitten and puppy had fallen asleep.

"I'll give you a hand unloading the wagon, Dad. Here, Mom, you take the puppy."

"No, son, you'd better take care of the puppy. They're both probably hungry," Enig said.

That night the kitten slept on the pillow with Blair and the puppy with Fergus. "You certainly made them happy, sweetheart. I have never seen them so happy. You did good."

In the morning Innis asked, "Have you two found names for your new friends?"

Blair said, "I think I'll call him Whiskers."

"And the puppy, Jack. Dad, what kind of a dog is Jack?"

"He's a beagle. He'd be good for hunting partridge and rabbits and he'll bark when an animal is too close to the house."

* * *

Before the snow was too deep in the woods, Enig cut enough trees to build a crib work in front of the house and at the high water line. It would be filled in with rocks later. He made steps in it and a wharf that extended out into the river and he filled that with rocks to prevent it from floating away.

Before spring, he had drawn up plans for a building to build boats in. "I'm going into town today to talk with Craig Randall at the blacksmith shop. You two can ride to school today."

"What can I do for you, Mr. McFarney?"

Enig laid out the plans for making a steamer, to bend wood for boats. "Can you make this, Craig?"

Craig studied the plans for a few minutes before answering. "Yes, it'll take me a while."

"Can you make it in three sections that'll bolt together when I have it in position?"

"That won't be a problem. How soon do you need it, Mr. McFarney?"

"Oh, by the end of August?"

"That gives me five months. I'll have it ready. You have my word on it."

"Thank you." From there he went to the sawmill and talked with Mr. Hall.

"Hello, Enig, what can I do for you today?"

"I need some more lumber. If you could deliver it May 1st," and he gave Mr. Hall the list of material.

"I see you are using 6x6 again."

"Yes, this is going to be a building to build fishing boats and no need to plane them."

"I don't see any problem. We have six weeks to make up

your order.

"Someday I'd like to come up and look at your house. No one around here has ever thought of using 8x8's."

"Come up anytime, Mr. Hall."

"Maybe my wife and I will walk up this weekend, weather permitting."

Before returning home, Enig picked up a few supplies for Innis and the newspaper. After lunch he sat down to read it. "What's going on in the world, Enig?" Innis asked.

"There's talk in here that the American Colonies are tired of British rule and dominance. Benjamin Franklin has recently returned from meetings in France and England. I can understand how they feel. That's the biggest reason I wanted to leave Scotland."

"Do you think it'll be resolved peacefully ... if it can't, this country just might declare war on England."

Jack barked once and scratched at the door. "He knows Fergus and Blair are home from school." When the door opened the cat, Whiskers, jumped off Blair's bed and ran out to her.

Sunday was a nice day and Cameron Hall and his wife Emily did walk out and visit. "This is nice, Enig. With eight inches of wood how does it heat?"

"Often times all we need is the cook stove."

"The walls are beautiful. What a marvelous idea. I wonder why no one has thought of it before now," Cameron said.

"It sure is easier than building with round logs."

Innis enjoyed having another woman to talk with.

CHAPTER 10

As soon as the ice and snow had melted and the river was free of ice, Enig and Fergus put the boat back in the water and tied it up securely to the new wharf. Then they started clearing the land where the boat shop would be.

With that done and while the ground was still soft, they began turning the sod over by hand for planting. They were all day and then another day raking the sod into piles and burying it in the garden soil. "The garden is ready for planting, Innis. Maybe you and Blair can do this while Fergus and I build the boat shop."

When the lumber was delivered, they were two weeks building it with ways on the inside to slide the finished boat to the water. And then they had to build the forms for bending the planks. They were finished three months before Mr. Randall would deliver the steamer.

"Son, I think it is time we went out and caught us a boatload of fish. I have already talked with Mr. Cummins at the store and he said he would try a load to see how well they would sell."

The fish were hitting the baited hooks and after six hours, they had caught two hundred pounds, which was all Mr. Cummings wanted for the first trip. So they pulled their lines and headed for Belfast.

Ralph Cummins paid them 5 pounds-6 shillings. "If these sell good, Mr. McFarney, I'll try another load."

At home they were still eating the last of the canned moose meat before it spoiled.

* * *

Enig checked with Craig Randall and the steamer would be delivered as they agreed. The next day instead of starting to build a boat, they had firewood to work up first. He wasn't sure how much wood it would take.

Then they had to provide the general store with another load of fish, mostly haddock this time.

"When are you going to start building a boat, Enig?" Innis asked.

"I wanted to start this summer, but there's firewood to get and Mr. Cummins said he could use a load of fish each week. And that brings in good money. Fish now before cold weather comes."

* * *

Fergus and Blair were back in school. "Today I'm going to remove that kidney shaped rock from the field."

He made a tripod with three sturdy spruce logs and suspended block and tackle from it. First he had to dig a tunnel under the rock so he could secure a rope under it.

Halfway under the rock, his spade hit something odd. It wasn't another rock nor the kidney rock. He cleared out dirt for a better purchase on the object. He could move it but he still couldn't see what it was.

He made the hole bigger so he could get down below ground level. Now he could grab it with both hands and when he was able to free it and pull it out from under the rock, he was dumbfounded. He was holding a small chest, about a foot and a half long, ten inches deep and eight inches high.

He sat down on the lip of the hole, holding the chest in his hands. He had no idea what he was holding.

He brushed the dirt off and carried it inside. "Innis!" No answer. "Innis!"

"What, what are you hollering about?"

"Innis, you'd better come here."

He set the chest on the table. "Where did you find that, Enig?"

"Under the rock."

"Under the rock? Well, are you going to open it or just look at it?"

He opened the lid and looked inside. There was a rolled up parchment . A scroll.

"What do you suppose, Enig?"

"I don't know." He took the scroll of parchment out and pushed the chest back. He sat there holding it and feeling the texture. "It feels like paper. Feel it, Innis."

She did, "It's softer than plain paper. Unroll it, Enig."

As he unrolled it he said, "It feels like newspaper." When he had it unrolled he laid it on the table flat.

They were both speechless for several moments. "What do you think, Enig?"

"It looks like old Scottish brogue. What do you think?"

"Like you, Enig, I can understand and speak a little but I never learned how to read or write it."

"It isn't only Scottish brogue, Innis; it's mixed with something else."

"I wonder how old it is? And who put it under the rock, Enig?"

"I don't know. I wish I did."

"I wonder if there is something else under the rock?"

"Let's go have a see, Innis."

He stepped into the hole and began pulling out more dirt from under the rock and feeling around with his hands. "There's nothing more here."

He began filling the hole in and pushing dirt back under the rock. When he had finished he began tamping the dirt to pack it. "I don't know why, Innis, but I don't think we are supposed to move this rock."

They sat on it talking about the scroll. He put his hand on the rock and he could feel a slight depression. He stood up and said, "Stand up Innis. I felt something in the rock."

"What did you feel, sweetheart?"

"It was a slight depression."

It was difficult to see it, so he ran his hand over the rock until he felt it again. "Here it is," and he pointed to it.

"I see it now. It looks like a small dimple."

"Put your finger on it, Innis."

She did and he stood back looking at the rock and walked around the rock looking and then he said, "It is exactly in the center of the rock."

Then he held his finger on it so Innis could see. "That had to have been put there by someone, Enig. I don't believe in coincidences."

"Neither do I. But who? When was it done?"

They walked back to the house and looked at the chest and scroll again. Innis was looking at the scroll while Enig was looking at the chest. "Look at this, Innis," and he passed the chest to her.

"Your first impression, Innis?"

"It's lighter than I would have thought."

"Exactly, this isn't wood or metal."

"What is it?"

"That's just it, I don't know. I have never seen anything like it before."

They sat at the table talking. "The strangest thing is that dimple is in the exact center of the rock. Being in the center, then it had to have been deliberately put there. That is not an act of nature," Enig said.

"I wish we could read old Scottish brogue. What if you could find someone who could, Enig?"

"Two reasons why we shouldn't. I don't think we should bring anyone else into this secret. And even if we found someone who could read old Scottish brogue, that person would never be able to decipher all the strange symbols and make any sense from it."

"So what do we do with it?" Innis asked.

Enig was silent for so long she thought he had not heard her. "Enig, what do we do with it?"

"There is only one thing we can do; we lock it in the chest and we must never say a word about what we have to anyone. Not even Fergus and Blair. Promise me, sweetheart."

"I promise."

"So do I."

Innis took everything from the chest and put the new chest in and covered it with old clothing they would not be needing. Then Enig locked it and put the key in his pocket.

* * *

Enig was busy enough and had very little time to think about the kidney rock and chest. For a few days after, they both did think of it on occasion, but it was soon forgotten.

Enig and Fergus had the shop building up and finished before August and after Mr. Randall delivered the wood steamer, so they geared up and went fishing. They both were surprised how fast they were catching haddock. Shortly after high noon they had to head back to Belfast.

"This is a beautiful catch, Mr. McFarney and I can give you 7 and a half pounds."

"Thank you, Mr. Cummins. Do you have any request for clams or lobsters?"

"I do have one request. Capt. McFee is scheduled here on the 10th. Last trip he asked if I could have fifty lobsters and four bushel of clams ready to go onboard. Do you think you and your son can fill that request?"

"We'll do our best, Mr. Cummins. You have a place to keep them until the 10th? We do not."

"Yes, out back."

"Well, we'll get right on it."

Enig gave his son 2 pounds for his help today. That evening the whole family dug clams on the sandy flats upstream until just before sunset. They filled a bushel basket. "What will we do with these, Enig?" Innis asked.

"Do we have any empty milk cans?"

"Yes, two."

"That'll do." It took both cans and they filled them with salt water after the clams were put in.

"What will we do with the lobster?" Innis asked.

"Well for now we could use the wash tub and dishpans. The water for the lobsters as well as the clams will have to be changed."

The first day out fishing for lobster didn't produce any. The next day only a few. Then on the third day, they caught thirty. "I think you and Blair should probably take what we have to Cummins' store. Fergus and I will continue clamming and fishing for lobster."

Two days before the 10th, Enig and Fergus had filled their request and Mr. Cummins paid them 12 pounds. And since the entire family had helped, the 12 pounds was divided up evenly. Blair was excited. She had never had any money of her own.

* * *

The blacksmith, Craig Randall, arrived as he said he would with a wagonload of parts. They had to make a couple of changes inside the shop to accommodate the steamer and boiler. "There," Craig said, "Delivered and installed. I guess you'll be in business soon."

"Thank you, Craig, you did an excellent job. It looks just like the one I left in Greenock."

Later, Innis asked, "When will you start building boats?"

"I'll get everything here that I'll need and I'll wait until it is too cold to fish on the open ocean. We should be able to make two during the winter."

Enig and Fergus made one more fishing trip out on the open ocean before school would begin. From their own wharf, Enig let his son pilot the boat. "I'm not going to tell you what to do, son, unless there is an emergency. You captain this trip." Sometimes Fergus would readjust a sail or something and Enig would have done it differently but he bit his lip and let his son figure it out. In the end he was pleased with Fergus' ability at thirteen.

After they had caught enough they started back. Fergus wanted to impress his dad and when he was close to the town wharf he maneuvered the sails and brought the boat in a three point landing. Only touching the wharf lightly.

"I'm impressed, son." Enig saw the smile on his face.

Even though Fergus had done a very good job sailing, he also knew he needed more experience before he would be comfortable letting him go out alone. *He's only thirteen,* he said to himself.

* * *

"Enig," Innis asked, "This year instead of a moose, could we get a pig? Roast pork would taste awfully good."

"Okay, and I can smoke some bacon. But we'll have to wait for cold weather."

Enig took a trip to town in the morning and dropped the kids off at school and then he went to see Cameron Hall at the mill.

"What can I do for you today, Enig?"

"I'm needing some hardwood. Do you have twelve inch wide ash boards?"

"We do and they should be dry."

"Good, here's a list of what I'll be needing."

Cameron looked at the list and said, "I have enough dry ash for this order also."

"When can you deliver?"

"Late this afternoon."

On rainy days when the weather wasn't fit to work outside

Enig started making the ribs for the boat. It was slow painstaking work, but he wanted every cut to be right. When he had enough for one boat, he cut out enough for another boat.

Once a week, if the weather was permitting, he would sail out to open water and fish for haddock.

One Saturday in the middle of October, the family went out in the marsh to pick cranberries, but found much of the marsh in water. Beaver had moved in and had built a large dam at the outlet end. There was a large house and a beaver packing mud on the side of it.

"Dad," Fergus said, "beaver pelts are worth good money."

"Yeah, but maybe we should let them be for a couple of years and there'll be more."

They were only able to pick two gallons of berries.

That evening as they were sitting in the living room talking, Innis asked, "Anything new at school?"

"There are two new students; brother and sister. The family moved here from New Brunswick," Blair said.

"What are their names?"

"Albon and Clare McGill."

"Good Scottish folks," Enig said.

"I'm hearing that the American colonies want to leave England's rule and form an independent country," Fergus said.

"That doesn't surprise me. I hope they succeed," Enig said.

* * *

Cold weather blew in after a dry snowstorm and Enig and Fergus went to town to buy a pig from Farmer MacDonald.

"How big a pig do you want, Mr. McFarney?"

"Oh, two hundred pounder at least."

He showed them to a pen and said, "Take your pick. Two and a half pounds."

It wasn't much trouble loading the pig into the wagon but they had to tie it in with rope. "He isn't happy, Dad."

"No and it's a good thing we don't have far to go. Thank

you, Mr. Mac Donald."

"If you need more I'll have a few during the winter."

They had to stop twice and tighten the ropes. At home and out behind the barn, Enig was fearing the pig might run off if they just let it lose, so he used another length of rope. Before he untied the ropes holding him in the wagon, he tied the other rope over his shoulders and between his front legs. Then he tied the other end to a tree. The pig was beginning to squeal up a storm. Innis and Blair came out back to see what was happening. "Sweetheart, you should probably take Blair back in the house. This isn't going to be anything she'll want to watch."

"Come on, Blair."

"Fergus, get me a ball peen hammer and my sharp butchering knife. I'll watch the pig." The pig had wound the rope around two smaller trees and it wasn't struggling as much now.

Fergus didn't know what was going to happen. "Give me the hammer, son, and as soon as the pig is down hand me the knife. And be quick about it."

Enig came in from behind the pig and hit it in the head with the hammer knocking it unconscious and he dropped. Fergus held out the knife. Enig took it and while the pig was still out he cut the throat and the jugular vein. Enig saw the expression on his son's face and explained, "When you butcher a pig you have to bleed it. I knock him out so he wouldn't feel his throat being cut. And the heart will still pump and pump the blood out, until he dies."

"Okay," is all Fergus could say.

They turned the pig so the head was downhill. "I'll stay here with the pig, if you would unhook the mule and back him up so we can hook on and drag the pig into the barn."

They hung the pig upside down and began skinning. "There's nothing as hard to skin as a pig. The hide is so tight to the flesh."

They cut the hide in three inch strips and skun those one

at a time.

When they were finished Fergus said, "That is some fine-looking meat."

Innis and Blair came out now. The gory work done, Enig handed her the pan with the heart and liver. "We'll have liver and onions tonight. Blair, will you get a bowl of potatoes?"

* * *

Jack would have some food to eat for a couple of months. Pork bones were soft and he would spend idle time chewing on them.

Blair's kitten was now fully grown and he proved to be an excellent mouser.

By the time Enig and Fergus put their boat away for the winter and were ready to start work on a new boat, Enig already precut many pieces and before Christmas they were ready to start framing the hull boards. "This steamer looks just like the one back home, Dad."

"It should, I took the plans for building it."

Working alone while Fergus was in school, progress on the boat was slow. By the middle of January, the hull was closed in and tight.

The finish work and rigging Enig could do a lot of alone and by mid-March the boat was finished.

Within a week, once people learned the boat was for sale, it sold and this encouraged Enig to start another. From the sale of the first boat, he paid Fergus.

Fergus was now fourteen with the same rugged build as his father. Blair was twelve and she was going to be a striking beauty in a few more years. Because her brother was earning money working with his father, Innis started paying Blair for her help around the house and for the clams she would dig every week.

Before the second boat was half finished, it was sold to Joseph Carr. It was completed in June. This gave Enig time during the summer to take care of the jobs around the house.

Innis noticed that Enig was more relaxed now, not always so uptight since the completion of the second boat. He now knew people here as well as back home in Scotland would want his fishing boats, once they knew where to find McFarney.

Each Sunday, weather permitting, they still had a family day with steamed clams and lobsters. "You know something, Enig, this new life here has turned out better than I would have imagined two years ago."

"Oh, we don't have as much money as we did in Greenock, but I, like you, like this life and I think the whole family is happier," Enig said.

In June, the *Venture* sailed into the Belfast harbor. Enig was in town and saw the familiar sails approaching. He concluded his business and waited for the *Venture*. He watched as the crew went about bringing in the sails and adjusting the rigging. As he reflected on his days at sea, he began to realize how much he had enjoyed that time. Before his mind started questioning if he had made the right decision to settle in Belfast and not take the position of chief bosun mate aboard the *Venture*, he saw Hew walking down the gangway.

"I was coming up to see you, Enig. Let's have a cup of tea in the mess."

Enig liked the feel of walking across the deck to the mess hall. It brought back fond memories. They sat at the captain's table and a cook brought the tea. "I understand you are back in the boat building business?"

"Yes, we built two this winter and I already have orders for two more."

"So I guess asking you to sail as chief bosun mate is out?"

"As much as I'd like to, I can't. I'm surprised how the sea got into my blood."

Hew laughed and said, "It happens to a lot of men. When some of them go ashore for good, they aren't worth a damn.

They can't get sailing out of their system."

"How has your business been, Hew?"

"We hardly get more than two days in any port, we're so busy."

"Hew, what are you hearing about the colonies wanting to separate from the Crown?"

"I think it will only be a matter of time and it will happen. I'm hearing more or less the same from both sides of the Atlantic.

"And that brings me to another matter. When we leave England on our next voyage, that will be the end for me."

"You quitting and coming ashore?"

"Not exactly. I'm quitting the Commonwealth for good. I intend to make my home port in Portland. I like the American Colonies and if trouble should start, I want to be on this side of the Atlantic. As a Navy officer, I would be required to serve His Majesty and I won't do that and fight the Americans."

"What about your crew?"

"I know more than half will stay with me. The others will have to find a ship home if they want to go back.

"I want to be settled here in this new country. I already have established shipping ties all up and down the east coast.

"How old is your son Enig?"

"He just turned fourteen."

"If he was older, I'd asked him to sign on as a bosun mate's apprentice, like you did on the *Queen Mary.*"

"If he was eighteen, I'd say yes. The time at sea would do him good."

"I'll ask again in four years."

They talked for an hour before Enig had to return home.

While Fergus and Blair were out digging clams, Enig told Innis what Hew had said, "Do you think there'll be any fighting?"

"Knowing England's vanity and ego—yes, I think that's a certainty."

He also told her about Hew moving to the Portland area.

"If Fergus was older, he would have wanted to sail with him as an apprentice to the bosun mate."

"When he turns eighteen and finished with school, I'd like to see him do a few years aboard ship. I did and I think it did me a lot of good."

Fergus and Blair came back carrying two buckets of clams. What they earned when the clams were sold was now their money.

Enig had had to employ more help and he rebuilt the workshop twice as big as it had been.

CHAPTER 11

Two more years had passed and the boat building business was now operating every month. They were producing four boats a year plus doing some repairs to other boats.

The McFarney name was well known in the fishing industry and orders were coming in from far away. Enig now had six full-time employees plus his son when he wasn't in school.

Blair was fourteen now and very pretty, just like her mother when she was fourteen. Fergus took after his dad, strong and muscular and stocky built. And at sixteen he commanded a natural authority. On weekends he and Blair would fish alone on the ocean and they kept the money from the sales.

One day in mid-morning in July a stranger walked from town to see Enig. "Mr. McFarney?"

"Yes."

"Mr. McFarney, I am Captain Horace Billdu on the *Carolina Queen*. I have a broken mast and Captain McFee told me to see you about replacing it."

"Well, Captain Billdu, let us have a look at it."

As they walked back to the docks, Capt. Billdu told Enig what had happened. "We were caught in a terrible storm off Cape Hatteras and the main mast began to splinter near the base. I had no choice but to order the main sails brought in. I met up with Capt. McFee in New York and he said if I could limp the ship to Belfast, you were the only man who could repair it."

Enig took one look at the mast and said, "This tree should

never have been used as a main mast."

"Why?" Captain Billdu asked.

"You see how this splinter follows the grain."

"Yes."

"See how it twists to the left and up."

"Yes."

"The wood grains aren't straight and a mast should be."

"Can you repair it?"

"Yes, but you'll be here in Belfast for a few days."

"Would the repair be quicker and less expensive than replacing the mast?"

"Quicker and about half the cost, and when I have finished it'll be stronger than new."

"Have at it then," Captain Billdu said.

Enig went to see Craig Randall at the blacksmith shop. "Hello, Enig, what can I do for you today?"

"Are you real busy?"

"Nothing that can't wait."

"I have a job for you on the *Carolina Queen* at the docks."

On the walk over Enig told him what he wanted.

After looking at the mast, Craig said, "This won't be any problem. I just need to know the circumference of the mast here and here."

"And Craig, I'll need you to make up four bolts to go all the way through."

Craig took measurements for the bolts also and said, "Enig, I would advise a third clamp also. A foot above where the splinter stops."

"Good point."

"I'll need a day to make the clamps and the most of a second day for the bolts."

"Okay, while you're doing that, I'll have a crew boring the holes through the mast."

Enig went back to his shop for some tools and lumber to

make a staging. "Fred, I have a repair job on a ship at the docks and I'll have to have two men. You have the shop until the repair is done."

He took Paul and Seth Harold, brothers. They were both good workers.

While Paul worked on boring the two bottom holes, Seth and Enig worked above him building a staging platform.

By the end of day the four holes were through the mast and just as Enig and his men were walking down the gangway, Craig pulled up with the three clamps.

They carried the clamps up and left them on the deck. "I'll bolt these in place tomorrow," Enig said.

Fergus was working every day in the shop during the summer. He enjoyed carpentry and building something and working with wood. Blair was busy helping her mother around the house, but she did get to take one day off during the week, plus on Sunday to dig clams. She was saving all of her money for a dowery.

Fergus was working the same as the crew. He was doing as much work.

The next day Enig, Paul and Seth had the three clamps bolted tight and in place before Craig arrived with the four bolts. "Any problem with the clamps, Enig?"

"No, they all fit like a glove."

"This has been a quick repair," Craig said.

"Yes, but we aren't done yet. We'll wind wet rope around the mast from the base to a foot above the top clamp."

"That's a good idea."

* * *

By noon the next day, they had the mast repaired and bound with rope and Enig went to see Captain Billdu. "We're finished, Captain. It didn't take as long as I first thought. From time to time, you might want to have the bosun check the tightness of the clamps and the bolts and retighten as necessary."

"How much do I owe you, Mr. McFarney?"

"70 pounds, Captain."

"That sounds excessive."

"Captain, if I had chosen to replace the mast with a new one, the mast alone would have cost you more than that."

"Yes, yes, you're quite right."

After paying the smithy, Craig Randall, Enig went home with a pocketful of money.

* * *

That fall of 1774, the *Venture* made another appearance in Belfast. "Innis, the *Venture* is in Belfast and I'm going down to talk with Hew and find out what is happening in the colonies."

The foreman, Fred Barring, had the shop again. Hew was on deck when he saw Enig approaching and he hailed him to come up.

"Thank you, Hew, for recommending me to Captain Billdu."

"I saw the repairs. Quite ingenious. That's why I recommended you. I still would like you to come aboard as chief bosun."

"We're hearing rumors Hew about America actually pulling out of the Commonwealth. Are they only rumors or is there more to it?"

"I don't know any particulars, but from what I have been told it is going to happen. And not too far in the future."

"So, where are you located now, Hew?"

"I bought a house in Cape Elizabeth. Right on the coast. The former owners were British Loyalists and they moved to New Brunswick."

"What about your original crew?"

"I kept all but two men. Both of them had families and chose to stay in Scotland."

"Do you still go back and forth from England and Scotland?"

"Right now only along the coast of America. This dispute is going to explode and when it does, I want to be on this side of the Atlantic. When it settles down, I may resume the old trade route."

"What are you loading this trip?"

"Potatoes, wheat, oats and bales of sheep wool. All going to New Haven, Connecticut. There I'll pick up armories for Boston and Portsmouth. The *Venture* is making good money now and so is the crew."

* * *

Enig and Innis talked often about what might happen in the near future. One day she asked, "Enig, what about the chest? What if we are overrun by the English? Surely we wouldn't want the chest and scroll to fall into their hands."

The next day they buried it under the kidney rock and they filled the chest with much of their money. For just in case.

* * *

The boat shop was still busy during the winter of 1775. Word of America declaring war against Great Britain didn't reach Belfast until a week later. "Well, it has begun," Enig said. "It's all over the newspaper."

The crew had just finished another boat but no other orders had come in and Enig had to lay off his men. Some volunteered to fight the Red Coats, as they were being called. Enig would have enlisted too, but he had a family to protect and he couldn't allow the chest to fall into enemy hands.

So he began fishing every day. "Tomorrow, Innis, I am sailing to Boston. I intend to fish on the way down to sell my catch in Boston. Then turn around and fish my way back to Belfast."

"I thought after talking with Hew, you had decided to go to New Haven, Connecticut," she said.

"I was, but New Haven is a long ways south of Boston and

I don't want to be away for so long. Not with America declaring war against Great Britain."

"How long will you be gone do you think?"

"I shouldn't think the round trip would take more than two weeks."

"Do you know of a fish market in Boston?"

"Yes, at least it was there on the waterfront, Harry's Fish Market, when I was sailing. I'm only assuming it'll still be there. "I'll be needing some water for me and some sandwiches."

"You should take Fergus with you."

"No, he needs to finish school and I'll feel better knowing he is here to protect the family."

He made his boat ready to leave in the morning with plenty of bait, line and hooks. Being in a small boat he knew he'd not be able to sleep. That he would have to sail during the night, so he made sure he had rain gear and wool blankets.

As the family were eating breakfast the next morning, Fergus said, "Dad, I think I should be going with you. That's a long trip and we could take turns sleeping."

"Thank you, son. Ordinarily I'd say yes. But these are strange times with a war happening in our backyard. I could sure use your help, but I'd feel much better knowing you are here to protect the family. While I'm gone you'll be the man of the house. I'm leaving my rifle for you. It is loaded. And at night keep Jack outside on his run. He's a good watch dog. He'll let you know if anyone is about."

The boat was tied up at their own wharf and they all walked with Enig to the wharf, Innis carrying a dozen ham and cheese sandwiches wrapped in paper.

"You two take good care of your mother and each other."

Innis wanted to cry, but she held back in front of her two children. Finally she said, "You be careful, sweetheart."

"I will," and he climbed aboard and as he raised the sails Fergus and Blair untied the ropes holding him to the wharf.

There was a breeze blowing down the Penobscot Bay and the sails filled with air and he was on his way.

He put his charts and sandwiches, wrapped in his raingear, under cover.

Once he was cleared of the bay, he let out two lines with only one baited hook on each line for now. He had sailed into a school of haddock right off and he was busy tending both lines. When there was a lull he cleaned them, leaving the heads on.

Just before he lost the sun for the day, he took a last sextant reading and then looked at his chart and decided he was off Portland. He had already pulled in both lines and now for the first time that day he ate three sandwiches and washed them down with water.

Fishing had been good; he already had a half a boatload. He hoped to fill it by the time he reached Harry's Fish Market in Boston.

He settled in for the night and wrapped a blanket over his shoulders and he pulled down his knit hat to cover his ears. With one hand on the tiller, he sat in silence with his thoughts, thinking mostly of family and the mysteries of the chest.

It was a cold long night. He allowed himself catnaps and he would check his compass often to make sure he was still on course.

A boatload of fish would bring good money and his family surely could use it, now the boat shop was closed because of the war.

He had to force himself to stop thinking about the chest and the scroll document inside. He knew he would never be able to decipher it and he didn't want to trust what it might have to say to anyone who might be able to read it. So to keep from going crazy, he forced those thoughts from his mind, and thought about his family.

There was a band of golden light along the northeastern horizon and as soon as there was enough light, he baited the hooks and tossed out the lines. Then he took a sextant reading and plotted it on his chart. There had been very little wind during the night, but he was surprised what he saw on his chart. He was a short distance north of Boston. He didn't want to go in with only a partial load, so he sailed in circles to fill his holds.

As he pulled in both lines, he was done fishing; he saw a ship with many sails bearing down on him. As it came close it was easy to see it was a British man-of-war.

Sails were lowered and the ship was slowing. It was obvious they intended to inspect his boat. He lowered his sails and waited.

They were close now and it should have been easy to see what he was doing.

"Ahoy there, who are you?"

"Ye kin numptie"—*Are you stupid?* He rolled his old Scottish accent as much as he could. He surely looked the part. He had grown a full beard during the winter and it was now solid gray, his knit hat pulled down on his ears. He pointed to his load of fish and said, "Keek"—*Have a little look.*

"Ahoy there, old timer. Where are you from?"

When he answered he really rolled the word Greenock. "Greenock, Scotland, laddie."

"Old timer, where are you going?"

"A nod's as guid as a wink tae a blind horse?"—*Explain yourself properly and make your meaning crystal clear.* "Ye kin numptie,"—*Are you stupid.*

"Are you carrying any guns, old timer?"

"Do yer dinger!"—expressing strongly his disapproval.

"Yer off ye rheid."—*You're off your head.* "You daft! I dinnae get only fish. Huvne no ken guni!"—*I don't have any guns.*

"Tis a dreich day on am a pare nick."—*It is a cold damp day and I am tired.* "Be off I weid ya. I go Harry's!"

"Captain, he's just a Scottish fishermen taking his catch to Harry's Fish Market," the first mate said.

"Let him go then."

Enig heard that and pulled his sails up and left, thinking how close that was.

Harry's was right where he remembered it being. It took two of Harry's men two hours to inspect and unload the fish. "That is a good catch, Mr. McFarney. I'll give you 20 pounds 6 shillings."

"Fair enough." If he remembered correctly, there was a tavern two blocks behind Harry's. He was hungry and he needed sleep. After eating a lunch of bacon and eggs and toasted biscuits and plenty of coffee—"You won't find any tea in Boston, mister, since the Tea Party."

"That's okay. I kinda like this coffee. I need a place to sleep."

"I have a room out back."

* * *

He didn't wake up until early the next morning. He heard doors slamming and men talking. He'd eat a good breakfast and leave.

"Good morning, Mr. McFarney. Breakfast?"

"Yes," he sat down with a cup of coffee. He noticed one of the men by the window kept looking at him. Uh oh, he's coming over now.

"Did I hear Mr. Savage call you Mr. McFarney?"

"Yes sir, you did. Enig McFarney,"

"May I join you?"

"Sit."

"Do you build the McFarney fishing boat?"

"I do."

"And you moved to Belfast, Maine, from Greenock, Scotland." Not a question.

"That's correct. Who am I talking with?"

Before answering the stranger looked around the tavern. "We have a common friend, Captain Hew McFee."

"I sailed three years with Hew onboard the *Queen Mary*. But that doesn't tell me who you are."

"I apologize, my name is Benedict Arnold."

"I know you by reputation. You have had your encounters with the British."

"Captain McFee tells me you are a terrific bosun mate and you recently repaired a main mast for Captain Horace Billdu."

"Yes, I did."

"Where are you going when you finish eating?"

"Back to Belfast."

"When do you plan to leave?"

"As soon as I finish eating."

"I would like to employ your services, Mr. McFarney."

"Tell me."

"I have a dispatch that must go north, and as far as I can see, the quickest route there would be via you."

"Where is the dispatch going?"

"The final destination I can not divulge. All you need to know is if you can get it to Belfast?"

"I can. And I doubt if you'll tell me what it is?"

"You're correct."

"What do I do with it once I am in Belfast?"

"Before I tell you anymore, I need to know if you'll carry it?"

"Yes."

"Okay, I have a contact in Belfast. He owns the general store."

"Ralph Cummins?"

"Yes. He does not know I have made contact with you, until you say, *The northern lights were bright last night.* That's all you have to say. After you have handed him the dispatch he knows to give you a 10 pound note.

"Now, when you are through eating, return to your room. I will be there."

Before leaving, Enig ordered two more eggs with biscuits

and more coffee. He was developing a taste for this coffee. When he finished eating and went to pay for his meal, Mr. Morris said, "Your friend has already paid for your breakfast."

"Thank you."

In his room, Arnold was indeed there waiting. "The safest way I have found to carry dispatches is on my back. Take your shirt off."

He did and Arnold had narrow strips of cotton cloth to wrap around Enig's chest and back securing the dispatch. "There, that should do it."

"I forgot to tell you, I was stopped by a British ship yesterday outside the harbor."

"What were they looking for?"

"Guns. I talked to them in the old Scottish brogue dialect and I don't know if they understood what I was saying or not. I think they were pretty annoyed with me."

"Good move. We may not meet again, Mr. McFarney, but if your services are needed again, someone will contact you. Goodbye and good luck," Benedict Arnold said.

* * *

The wind was good and Enig had full sail catching the wind, and he was moving fast, now that he was empty, and riding high in the water. Off in the distance, he could see the big sails of the English man-of-war ship and he knew as long as he maintained full sails, the man-of-war would never be able to catch him.

It was a bright, starlit night, and he kept his boat pointed for home waters. There was an urgency to get this dispatch to the drop off and he didn't run any lines out until the next morning.

He knew he was making good time and he pulled up to his own wharf about 3 a.m. Jack started barking, Fergus came out with the rifle to see what was going on and he was surprised, "Dad? Is that really you, Dad? You're back a week early."

"Hello, son, good to see you're on the ball. Let's go in."

By now everyone else was up. "Why are you back so early, Enig?" Innis asked. "Did you fish at all?"

"I had a full load by the time I arrived at Harry's Fish Market in Boston. I have never seen the fishing so good. And he paid me three times what Ralph Cummins would have. On the return trip the fishing wasn't as good and being empty, with a fair wind I made good time.

Then he told them about the English man-of-war ship. "She was huge and ugly. There were cannons sticking out everywhere. I used the old Scottish brogue when I talked with them and of course they couldn't understand me and eventually they let me go."

"Are you hungry, Enig?" Innis asked.

"Yes, but I need sleep first."

Everyone back to bed. When Enig took his shirt off Innis said in surprise, "What have you on your back?"

"I had forgotten that was there. I can't tell you much. It's something to do with this war. I'm to deliver it tomorrow. I have no idea where it will be going from here, nor what it says. And you can't ask me any questions. You must trust me, sweetheart."

"Okay."

* * *

He was awake two hours later and after a hurried breakfast, he and Fergus sailed the boat down to the docks. "Mr. Cummins, is there someone who can help Fergus unload the boat?" Before Ralph could answer, Enig said, "The northern lights were bright last night."

Ralph motioned with his head towards the back room, then he went out front and told his helper to help Fergus unload the boat.

"You have something for me, Enig?"

Enig handed him the package and Ralph gave him a 10 pound note. "When will you be making another trip to Boston, Enig?"

"Two weeks, weather permitting."

Out front Ralph paid him for the load of haddock, and Enig and Fergus started back up the river for home. Just as they were tying up at their wharf, someone in a canoe was going hell bent for election up river. Enig figured that was probably the final destination of the dispatch he had brought from Boston.

He handed Innis the money, for both sales of fish and the 10 pound note. "Wow, how much fish did you sell in Boston?"

It wasn't lunch time yet, but Enig said, "I could eat another breakfast. And here," he handed Innis a two pound package of coffee. "Tea can't be purchased anywhere now after the Tea Party. People are drinking this instead."

"What is it?"

"Coffee, and here's a coffee pot I found at Cummins store." He showed Innis how much of the grounds to use, "...and then set it on the stove to boil."

"How long do I boil it?"

"That, I don't know. You'll have to experiment."

She let the first pot boil a bit too long and Enig had put in a bit too much grounds. "It's different," Innis said.

After eating, he went back down to the boat and began cleaning it. Then he started looking for a place to hide dispatches if he was ever boarded and searched.

The best place to hide anything is in plain sight. So he dismantled his seat at the tiller and made a hidden compartment under the cushion. When he had finished, he was feeling better. It was time for supper.

* * *

While he was gone, the rest of the family had put in the garden. While Enig was looking at the garden, Innis and Blair had taken the mule and wagon to town. When she came back she said, "Enig, Mr. Cummins said since the war started there aren't as many fishermen and he could really use some haddock. He said he was out."

Enig and Fergus went fishing while Innis and Blair dug clams. Blair didn't have as much opportunity as her brother to earn money, so all the clams they dug were Blair's to sell. She was happy.

It was late afternoon before Enig and Fergus returned to Cummins Store with almost a full load.

Before leaving they both bought new gloves. As they were going out the door, Cummins said, "Will you be here early tomorrow morning, Enig? I understand the northern lights will be bright tonight." Enig only nodded his head.

Before dark, Enig prepared the boat for another trip to Boston. "I wish I could go with you, Dad," Fergus said.

"I know, son, but I need you here."

"I'll work on firewood."

In bed Innis asked, "Do you know what you'll be carrying?"

"No, I hope it is only dispatches like before."

The next morning at the breakfast table, Enig asked, "Fergus, there is something I'd like you to do while I'm away. Talk with Craig Randall at the blacksmith shop and ask him if he can make a little stove for the boat. It would be awful nice if I could warm up a sandwich and make a pot of hot coffee. The nights are cold and long."

"Okay. Dad, you know the mule is getting old. Maybe we should think about getting another."

"Okay, talk with Clyde McDonald. Your mother has enough money. Or Mr. Randall might have something."

"I'll check."

Enig hugged Innis and kissed her and hugged Blair and shook his son's hand like a man. "I'm proud of you, son—all of you."

* * *

"I'm glad to see it is only dispatches again and nothing bulky."

"Have a good trip, Enig, and catch me another load of haddock."

As soon as he could, he put both lines out and this time he had two baited hooks on each line. And like before, he sailed over a large school of haddock and he was extremely busy pulling in his lines, most of the time they each were supporting two haddock. And like before, he was out of the school and things slowed. Not stopped, but slowed.

Eventually he came to another school and this one lasted longer. When it slowed, he took a moment to eat a sandwich. He looked off to the left and saw huge sails. It wasn't any fishing boat. Probably the same English man-of-war ship. *I wonder if they'll shadow me to see what I'm doing or be on their way.*

He finished his sandwich, and decided this would be a good time to take a sextant reading. At least he'd be able to tell someone the English were patrolling off the Maine coast.

Two hours later, the English ship was much closer. The English Captain said, "Lieutenant, what have you to starboard?"

"It looks like that same old Scot fisherman we saw ten days ago, Captain."

"We'll come a bit closer to make a positive identification."

"Yes Sir."

Enig could see he was being watched through a telescope. He waved and kept pulling in haddock.

"Captain, I have positively identified him as the same old grizzled Scot and he is fishing."

"No sense trying to talk and understand him. Set your course for New York, Lieutenant."

"Yes Sir."

As they veered off to port the lieutenant was still watching and saw the old grizzled Scotsman wave.

Enig was feeling pretty good. He logged the encounter; time, longitude and latitude and their direction of travel.

As he continued on to Boston, he kept wondering where the English had come from. Perhaps Nova Scotia, patrolling the east coast.

It was another cold night. He'd pulled in both lines before dark, a north wind had come up and he was making good time. There was enough moonlight so he was able to check his compass occasionally.

Before mid-afternoon the next day, he had finished filling his boat. The sun was setting as he pulled into Harry's wharf. The first thing he did was see Harry.

"Hello, Mr. McFarney. Back so soon?"

"Yes, the northern lights were bright last night and I was able to make good time. Come out and look at my catch, Harry."

Harry followed him out and said, "I'll have to get a couple of men to help me with the fish." All the time Enig was retrieving the dispatch from under his seat, he told him about seeing the English warship; the longitude and latitude and how many sails she had and in which direction she was sailing.

"Come in, Mr. McFarney, you must be hungry," and he palmed a 10 pound note into Enig's hand.

While Enig ate beef stew and biscuits two men unloaded his boat. Harry gave him another 20 pounds- 6 shillings.

"You can have the same room as before."

"Thank you, Harry. What is your last name?"

"Better if you didn't know."

* * *

There were no dispatches going back and a day out from Boston he came onto more schools of haddock. He didn't know if Ralph Cummins could handle a full load or not, so he stopped fishing when his boat was half loaded.

He pulled in to the wharf in Belfast at 8 p.m. He helped Ralph's men unload the fish. He left his boat tied up at the wharf and walked home.

The next day Fergus showed his dad the little stove the smithy had made. "He had to use some special sheet metal that he had and it was expensive. But he hopes you'll like it."

It was about the size of a nail keg on a stand with a flat

surface on top for a pot or a kettle. "This will do, son. How much?"

"5 pounds and 4 shillings."

Enig wanted to see the new mule. "How old is he, son?"

"Two, and Blair and I have been riding him."

"We'll probably have to buy extra feed this winter."

CHAPTER 12

Enig didn't have to make another trip to Harry's until September. And he was glad for the new stove. He saw the same English man-of-war ship and it paid little attention to him. This dispatch originated from inside Nova Scotia and New Brunswick from people who wanted to see England defeated.

On his return, he carried another dispatch, that would be relayed all the way to Castine, Bangor, Saint John, New Brunswick and Halifax, Nova Scotia. But he had no idea what the dispatches said. He was a mule.

Things were quiet around Belfast in the winter of 1776, and the boat shop, too, was quiet. Enig had earned enough money fishing and delivering dispatches so the family was okay. He kept himself busy with finding food for both mules and cutting firewood.

He was also making plans in his head to enlarge the boat shop and some improvements to the house.

Come spring in 1776, Enig and Fergus continued fishing. They were the only suppliers now for Ralph Cummins. Enig had kept watch all winter for the *Venture* and he was wondering if perhaps he had encountered that English warship or another. Then in the middle of April, he saw familiar sails approaching Belfast. He waited on the docks for his friend.

The crew immediately started dismantling some of the rigging and main sails. "Hello, Hew, what's going on with the crew?"

"Good to see you, Enig," and they shook hands. "I understand we have a mutual friend."

When Enig didn't respond, Hew said, "General Benedict Arnold." That's all that was said.

"What are you doing here, Hew?"

"Can't you see? My main mast. It needs some serious repairs. Come up and look at it and see if you come up with an idea how to fix it."

"What happened?"

"I'll tell you when we won't be disturbed."

"There's a section missing from the center of the mast." He walked around the deck looking at the remaining mast and rigging. Then he went below to look at the mast anchor.

"The mast anchor is okay. No splintering or cracks. Let's go back on deck. I want to look at the mast again."

"This will have to be cut off eight feet above the deck and a seven foot splice made, and on the end of a new mast. Staging will have to be built. Let's go see what the harbor master has for masts. I know he has a few."

By the end of that day, Captain McFee's men had the staging built and the old mast all cut off eight feet above the deck. The top damaged piece was lowered to the deck and then moved to the docks.

"Hew, we're done here for the day. Come to supper with the family."

As they walked home, Hew told Enig how the mast was broken. "A cannon ball hit it and that's all it hit. None of my men were injured."

"Okay, Hew, tell me what you are doing to warrant being fired on."

"I am employed by the New United States Continental Congress to seek out British ships and log information about them. Harass them whenever possible and carry provisions to different ports.

"A week ago I had just left Boston and we spotted an English man-of-war sailing south. Probably to New York or looking for enemy ships to engage. The *Venture* is a sleek ship and she is much faster than any of the British gun ships.

"If they have a favorable wind, I'll get in behind them and pursue. There are two long range cannons on the bow and one aft. The English warships also have cannons aft.

"It's difficult to turn the port or starboard cannons to fire behind them, so I quarter in to them from the rear. I have two good cannon men on the bow and they seldom miss. We haven't sunk any ships yet, but we have wreaked havoc on six.

"After we have done enough damage, I veer off and leave, and they are too crippled to give chase.

"You probably noticed the *Venture* has more sails now. That and a sleek design to the ship gives us a tremendous advantage over the enemy.

"I think I would have made a pretty good pirate," Hew said.

"It is good to see you again, Innis, and you, too, Fergus and Blair. My, how you both have grown.

"Innis these beans are delicious." For dessert they had apple pie and cheese.

"I hate to eat and run but I really must get back to my ship. See you in the morning, Enig?"

"Yes, I'll be there."

* * *

Fergus went to work the next morning with his dad, since it was Saturday and there was no school. He helped his dad mark off the vertical cut down the mast for the splice and they nailed on boards at the edge of the line to help guide the saw blade. Then they measured the diameter at the top and found the same diameter on the new mast and marked it. They cut off the seven foot end and laid out the marks for the splice on the end.

By noon, both ends of the splice were cut and planed

smooth. After lunch, Craig Randall showed up to measure the mast where the clamps would go and how long the four bolts would have to be.

"There isn't much more we can do today, Hew. The smithy will probably have the iron ready tomorrow morning; at least the clamps. Then we can raise the new mast and set it in place. Did your men put rope to soaking?"

"Yes."

The next morning Enig found the smithy had already been there and had left the clamps. "Just to make the job go faster and easier, Fergus, would you start boring the holes through this half of the splice. I'll get someone to help you."

Fergus and his two helpers were two hours boring the four holes.

The ropes had already been attached to the mast and Hew's crew began lifting the new mast with the onboard booms and tackle. By 10 o'clock the mast was in place and the three clamps bolted as tight as they could get 'em.

By early afternoon, Craig Randall arrived with the four bolts. The crew still had one more hole to bore.

When the bolts were tightened as much as they could be tightened, and the same with the clamps, Hew stood back on the aft deck looking at the new mast. "It's straight and looks good!" he hollered.

"The rest is up to your crew, Hew, to get the rigging back up and the sails."

"You are a good carpenter, Enig. Thank you. How much do I owe you?"

"You can pay my son for his work, but me, *nah*. You don't owe me anything. My contribution to the war effort."

Hew gave Fergus 2 pounds, and he was happy.

"When will you be leaving, Hew?"

"Just as soon as the sails are up. We have more English ships to disrupt."

"Be careful, Hew."

As Enig and his son were loading up the wagon, Fergus said, "Dad?"

"Yes, son?"

"I'm glad Hew didn't ask me if I still wanted to sail with him as a bosun apprentice."

"What made you change your mind?"

"Well, it wouldn't be maritime shipping; it would be war. Battles at sea."

"I was glad he didn't bring it up either."

"There is something else, Dad."

"Go on."

"Three other boys at school and I have been talking about this. There is a militia group forming in Belfast and from the neighboring villages, to protect our town. And I want to be part of that." He left it there waiting for his dad to say something.

"As I said, I'm glad Hew didn't ask you to sign on. I understand. And at the same time, I understand why you want to join the militia. I think it is a good idea.

"You don't have to tell me, Dad, but I know these fishing trips to Boston, aren't only about catching haddock. I've watched you at home and you have changed some. And then there is the boat seat you made to conceal something. You're doing your part and I want to do mine."

"Fair enough, son."

* * *

Fergus finished his schooling and was given his certificate. The group forming a local militia group told him and his two friends, Daren Sibley and Mike Downs, that they would have to provide their own rifle; Belfast would provide shot and powder. Sibley and Downs both already had their own rifles and Fergus bought the last rifle Mr. Cummins had in his store.

There wasn't any training and the band of twenty-five young men were led by Captain Fred Ames. He had recently resigned from the British Army stationed outside of Boston. He now hated the British. "The dirty Red Coats," as he was calling them.

He knew his men obviously knew more about wilderness survival, but he knew and understood the Red Coats—a really good combination.

Their first maneuver was to make a wide circle around Belfast, and circle to the north and meet up with another militia doing the same out of Searsport.

After a day of rest, they repeated the maneuver in the opposite direction and a wider circle. They met up with a scouting party of Red Coats halfway between Morrill and Belfast. Two of the enemy were killed, three received slight flesh wounds and they captured five more. The Belfast Regulars, as they were calling themselves, had only suffered one man with a shoulder wound.

Not wanting to break off the detail, Captain Ames ordered Fergus, Sibley and Downs to escort the prisoners to Belfast and the wounded for medical treatment in Belfast.

The Red Coat prisoners had to help their own wounded on the march and Stanley Smith was doing okay for the first two hours, then he was feeling faint and slowing down. Fergus carried him over his shoulder and Sibley carried his pack and rifle. Downs was watching the prisoners.

"Hang on, Stan, we're on my family's land now and we'll be at my home soon."

* * *

"Blair, go see what Jack is barking about. It can't be your father, he is in the boat shop."

Jack was really barking up a storm now. Enig and Innis came out to see also. "Don't let Jack go, Blair. It might be a bear."

Then they heard a familiar voice, "Hello, there at the house!"

121

"My word!" Innis exclaimed, "It's Fergus and he's carrying someone on his shoulder."

"He isn't alone, Mom. There's more coming in behind him," Blair said.

"Mom, we have four men here that are going to need some attention. Stan, here, is the worst. He has a shoulder wound. The others are only flesh wounds."

"Bring Stanley in the kitchen. The others can stay on the porch. Blair, I'm going to need your help. First get me some hot water and then take his shirt off. I'm going to wash my hands."

"I'll tend to the wounded on the porch," Enig said.

"Fergus, there is hot food on the stove. Feed the men," Innis said.

All Enig had to do for the flesh wounds was to clean them out and tie a bandage around them.

"What happened, son?"

"We were on a scouting patrol between Searsport and Morrill and ran into an enemy patrol."

"Did you lose anyone?"

"No, and Stan was the only one wounded. Three of the enemy were killed."

"Wow, I had no idea the British were so close. I'm glad you men were out there."

After Fergus had taken out a kettle of beef stew, he went back inside. "How is he, Mom?"

"All I can do is clean out the wound. He needs a doctor and soon," Innis said.

"I'll go out and hitch up the mule and wagon," Enig said.

After they had Stan in the wagon, Enig said, "I'll take him in to see Doc Abrams."

"No Dad, this is my job now. You stay home with the family." Enig smiled and nodded his head.

"We'll march these five in behind you. Fergus," Sibley said.

After Sibley and Downs left with the five prisoners, Enig, Innis and Blair sat on the porch. Blair was the first to break the silence, "Well, there went our supper."

"I'll fry up some bacon and eggs," Innis said.

Enig was still thinking how much Fergus had already changed when he told his father, *No I'll take him to the doctor, you stay here with the family.* He didn't say anything until later when he and Innis were in bed. "He's a man now, sweetheart. We don't have to worry anymore."

CHAPTER 13

Capt. Ames of the Belfast Regulars soon saw a leadership ability with Fergus McFarney. Everyone liked him and they all looked up to him for support and answers. So a month after the brief battle with the enemy scouts, the captain promoted Fergus to sergeant.

The militia kept busy patrolling from Northport to Searsport, and only on rare occasions were the enemy ever seen and engaged.

Once a week, weather permitting, Enig would spend a day fishing. Mr. Cummins was still paying the same. Twice a year Enig would have to make a trip to Boston with dispatches and on these runs he would deliver a boatload of fish to Harry's Market.

A ship damaged by the English man-of-war ship arrived in Belfast with damaged masts, and Enig would be employed to make the repairs.

Two more years of fighting for independence, and it still continued. The Continental Army would win a few battles and the British would win a few. But what England thought would be an easy, quick war had dragged on now for three years with no end in sight.

Although Enig still was not building any fishing boats, he was making improvements to his shop, so once he was back in business there would be new improvements. He now had two ways for launching boats from the shop to the water.

He improved the steamer and made another jig for bending

the hull boards. In a corner of the shop, he made a hearth for smelting his own iron.

When he had done all he could to the shop, he began looking at the house for improvements.

Two years ago, Blair discovered she had a natural ability for medicine when her brother had brought the wounded in from a recent battle.

She had finished school and now she was working for Doctor Abrams, starting out only helping to make patients comfortable, but Dr. Abrams slowly began introducing her to more nursing duties. She was excited to be learning how to help and comfort people and she now was earning her own money.

"What are you working on now, Enig?" Innis asked.

"How would you like a brick fireplace on this south wall?"

"It would be nice. But what would we do with the Franklin fireplace?"

"We might build an addition."

"Why would we add on?"

"When this fighting is over, Fergus will be back and sometime he'll marry and have a family and I think this would be a good place for his family with the boat shop right here also."

"Okay, it would be nice to have grandchildren running around."

"I have another reason also."

"Oh, and what?"

"I'll make a place to put a safe, to keep the chest and our money in."

"I would think a rock fireplace would look better," Innis suggested.

"It would be more work, but it wouldn't cost as much."

They found plenty of rocks along the shore between home and Belfast. When Innis wasn't doing housework or baking, she helped Enig with the rocks.

One drizzly day he walked to town to talk with Craig

Randall at the blacksmith shop. "What can I do for you today, Enig?"

"I'm building a stone fireplace and I need some grates made from three inch iron pipes, so the air will flow up through the pipes and out." He drew Craig a rough sketch.

"I can do that, Enig, and from the tops of the tubes that form the grates, they will have to be threaded, and elbows, 45° or 90° added on as needed. When do you need them?"

"I haven't started building it yet. We have been busy hauling in rocks from the shoreline. Maybe in a week?"

"How many pipes do you want?"

"Four."

"Work has been slow since the war started, but I can have it for you in a week."

"Thank you, Craig."

From there he went to the general store. "Mr. Cummins, I'm looking for a safe. Would you have any?"

"No, I don't. I sold the only one I had to Mr. Hall at the mill last week. I know he was going to sell the old one. It might be something you'd be interested in."

At the mill, Mr. Hall said, "Good morning, Enig. What are you building now?"

"A stone fireplace. I was just talking with Mr. Cummins at the general store and he said you have a safe you would like to sell."

"I do; it's out back. Follow me and we'll go look at it."

"It's a corner safe. I don't know if you'd be interested in something like this or not."

"Will you open it? I'd like to see how much space there is."

"It isn't locked, just pull the door."

The chest would fit very nicely. "It's just what I need. How much, Mr. Hall?"

"6 pounds."

"This is what I'll do, Mr. Hall. I'm not ready for it yet. But when I am if you would have two men deliver it, I'll give you 8 pounds now."

Enig paid him and they shook hands and Cameron Hall gave him a slip of paper with the safe's combination.

From there he went to the foundry and bought lime and gypsum to mix in with clay for mortar to cement the rocks together. Then he went back to the general store and bought a wheelbarrow and a wash table to mix the mortar.

* * *

Before he could start the fireplace, he had to cut through the floor and build a base to support the weight, since the stone would be all inside except for the chimney that went through the roof.

He was a week doing that, and one day Innis took the mule and wagon to town and she brought back the pipe grates.

Enig discovered masonry wasn't like carpentry where you could walk on it as soon as it was built. With masonry, he had to do a little each day and let the mortar set up without going too high with the stones.

After three weeks, after the base was made, he had it up and through the roof and tight to the weather.

"Are you going to put the chest in the safe?"

"That was my intention from the start. But if the British happen to take over Belfast, they'll probably steal everything they can carry off. Maybe we'd be better off leaving it under the rock. Only you and I know about it."

"Besides," Innis added. "How long has it been under the rock now—no one knows. It's safe there."

"When can we build a fire in it to see how it'll heat the house?" Innis asked.

"We'll have to wait until the mortar is good and dry."

"It looks nice, sweetheart, and I like how you made the hearth on both sides all the way to the outer walls," she said.

127

* * *

Blair didn't make it home every afternoon. Sometimes there were patients that required her assistance and she swapped off every other weekend with another nurse. She had seen the fireplace under construction. But when she came home that weekend, she was surprised to see it finished and how nice it looked. "That looks a lot better than that iron fireplace stove."

Whiskers heard her voice and she came running out from Blair's bedroom and jumped into her arms, purring.

"Have you heard or seen anything of Fergus?" Blair asked.

"Not since he dropped in for a few minutes two weeks ago. Have you heard anything about the regiment?" he asked.

"Not a word."

"You know, sweetheart, we have only seen Hew once after you repaired his mast. I hope he is alright," Innis said.

"I think he'll do just fine."

The following Monday morning another tall mast ship pulled into the docks at Belfast. And they, too, had mast damage from canon fire from an English man-of-war that had retreated from the battle because of more extensive damage.

Enig could see the tall sails from his wharf and went in to speak with his wife. "There is another tall mast ship that just pulled into Belfast. I'm supposing he needs some repairs. If not, I'll be back soon. I'll take a mule and wagon in case I have to come back for tools."

This was a Continental Congress warship, the *Spirit of America*. From the bridge, Captain John Freeman bellowed, "I'm Captain John Freeman of the *Spirit of America* and I am looking for Enig McFarney."

The captain's. bellowing irritated Enig and he said, "Stop your bellowing. I'm Enig McFarney."

"Come aboard."

The captain met him at the top of the gangway. "Now, Captain, what can I do for you?"

"I have a splintered main mast and the forward jib mast is broken in two. Can you do the repairs?"

"I'll need to look at the main mast," and he left the captain standing there and walked off to look at the mast.

"You come highly recommended, Mr. McFarney, by Captain McFee."

"How is the captain, sir?"

"I talked to him in the port of Baltimore a week ago and he said you were the best man to make these repairs. Oh, and he said to say hello."

A cannon ball had hit the mast eight feet above the deck, splintering the top portion. "The top will have to be replaced. I'll need some of your men to help, Captain."

"You tell me what you need and it is yours."

"Okay, first I want your men to build a sturdy staging eight feet high, so we can cut the top portion away. While your men are building the staging I need to get my tools from home and talk with the smithy about making some clamps and bolts. I'll be back in two or three hours."

He loaded his tools in the wagon and explained to his wife what he would be doing. From there he went to the blacksmith shop. "I want to put four clamps on this one, Craig, since the mast is taller. And the three bolts. We should have the top section cut away by one o'clock, if you want to come and take some measurements. I want two clamps below the cut and two above. I'll probably be at Hall's mill looking at a new mast, so if I'm not there, help yourself."

The ship's bosun had his crew build the staging and they were now taking the jib mast down. "Bosun, have your men hook onto the top section of the mast and support it while we cut through. Use two booms so the cutoff section doesn't get to swinging once it is free.

Captain Freeman stood back, approving of how Mr. McFarney was handling the job.

By the end of the day, the old section of the mast was now laying on the deck and the splice cut on the remaining section was made and planed smooth. Craig Randall had taken the measurements he needed and returned to his shop.

"Captain Freeman, you and I need to go to Hall's mill and find another mast."

"We have several out in the yard now, Enig," Cameron Hall said.

They found one with the exact butt diameter as the top of the bottom section of the old mast. They were able to cut ten feet off the top.

"It will still be a heavy lift, Captain. We'll need two booms to lift it and another boom on each side to steady and guide it into place."

Craig Randall took measurements on the new mast for the clamps and bolts.

"By mid-afternoon, I should be able to have two clamps done. The bottom and the top clamp."

It was getting late in the afternoon and all Enig had time to do was inspect what the men had been doing. When he was satisfied he said, "I'll be here shortly after first light, Captain."

On his way home, Enig marveled at how well disciplined the crew were and all were willing to help.

He was tired and shortly after supper he went to bed.

Innis was happy he was working again.

* * *

Cutting the splice on the new mast and setting it in place went off like clockwork. By the time the men had tightened the two clamps, Craig Randall delivered the last two. "Give me twenty-four hours to have the bolts made."

With the four clamps now secured to the repair, "Bosun, I'll need enough rope to wrap the splice."

"Would salt water be okay?" Bosun asked.

"Yes, no problem."

The splice was bolted and the rope was wrapped tightly around it. The bosun and his men had repaired the smaller jib mast.

Cameron Hall, Craig Randall and Enig McFarney were all paid with Continental Congress vouchers. "Where do I collect money for this voucher, Captain?" Enig asked.

"From the government, when this war is over."

Craig Randall was standing with Enig on the docks watching the *Spirit of America* sail away. "Do you think we'll see any money, Enig?" Craig asked.

"We may, once this war is over. If we win"

* * *

By the spring of 1781, the Red Coats influence had been removed from the entire territory of Maine. The British soldiers were too accustomed to facing their enemy on an open battlefield and not guerrilla warfare, where the enemy hid behind trees. The British outnumbered the local militia, but they didn't compare with their savvy and ingenuity. And the Red Coats were not used to the extreme winters or the spring blackflies.

Fergus had seen his share of fighting and word was circulating throughout all the troops that the British couldn't hold out much longer.

Blair had met a young doctor and they were married and had moved to Bangor.

On October 30th, 1781, Enig picked up a newspaper from the general store and folded it up and put it in his back pocket. When he finished his business in town, he walked home.

Tea still could not be purchased, and Enig and Innis had developed a taste for coffee. She had made a fresh pot and met Enig on the porch with a hot cup and they sat down.

Enig sipped his coffee and unfolded the newspaper. "Holy cow, Innis! The war is over!"

"What did you say?"

"The war is over. On September 29th the American forces

attacked General Cornwallis at Yorkstown, Virginia. The battle lasted for twenty days and finally on October 19th, Cornwallis surrendered, ending England's rule over the American colonies. Six and a half years and the war is finally over."

"Oh, I hope Fergus will be home soon," Innis said.

The first thing they did was to dig under the rock and retrieve the chest and put it in the safe.

Two days later, Fergus came walking up the road with a big grin on his face. He saw his dad walking towards the barn. At first there was very little said between them. "Welcome home, son," Enig was finally able to say.

"Innis! Innis, Fergus is home!"

She came running out of the house wiping her hands on her apron.

"Are you hungry, son?"

"I could eat a mule."

"What about ham and eggs?"

He drank two cups of coffee while his mother was frying eggs and ham. "What about Daren Sibley and Mike Downs? Did they make it?"

"Yes, we never lost a man. There were a few wounds but no casualties. Captain Ames was one helluva soldier. He kept us together.

"Well, Dad, when do we start building boats?"

This is what Enig wanted to hear.

CHAPTER 14

It took Fergus two days to get acclimated back to home life before he and his dad opened the shop for business. Innis wrote a letter to Blair and her husband, Dr. Clarence Hagan.

"I like the changes you made with the shop, Dad."

"Once we get moving, the changes should simplify things."

"I see you have plenty of firewood. Do you need anything else done before winter?"

"I think we are okay. Do you feel up to working? I'd like to get started tomorrow."

* * *

Just the two of them working they had the boat half built by the end of November. Two orders came in, in early December and Enig went to town to hire help. His old foreman, Lain Frasier, came back to work as well as two other men that had worked there before the war. A week later he hired two young men who had finished school in the spring. The first boat was finished by the end of December and Enig sailed it down to the docks.

The buyer was there to meet him and paid him.

After the new year, the United States Navy, as it was being called, sent several ships to Belfast during the year of 1782, that had sustained damage during the war. And Enig was being paid in the new US currency, and he was also paid for his voucher. The English pound currency was still accepted everywhere.

By the end of that year, the McFarney Boat Company had

built four boats and repaired four US Navy tall mast ships.

One day in the spring of 1783, Enig left Fergus and Lain Frasier in charge of the shop, and he and Innis sailed up the river to Bangor. They exchanged their English pounds for dollars and spent the night with Blair and her husband.

* * *

As busy as the boat shop was, it became obvious they needed a much bigger building and the area around the house was not large enough or suitable, so Enig inquired about buying a strip of land from home to Belfast. All he wanted was a strip which included the road and an acre next to town for the new building.

"Land is cheap right now Mr. McFarney. I can let you have what you want for $50.00," the land agent Gilbert Thomas said.

"You make out a deed, Mr. Thomas, and I'll have your money here shortly after lunch."

"Son, can you and Lain handle things here? I want to get started on this new building and I don't want to pull men out of the shop. I'll hire local men to build it."

The new building was big enough to support the building of four boats at the same time on four different ways, and when finished the boats would launch directly into the bay.

While the building was going up, Enig talked with Craig Randall about building a bigger and more efficient steamer. He also made new and improved jigs for forming the rails and hull boards.

He had the smithy build a small furnace for bending iron.

It took a year to finish the new shop and move everything from the old shop.

By 1785, Fergus more or less was in charge of the shop now. Enig was spending time with Innis taking care of the homestead, but he did go in each day. And when a big ship arrived with a damaged mast or rigging, Enig took charge of those repairs.

The Bangor National Bank had set up a small branch bank

in Belfast now, and the company was keeping accounts there, as were most people in the area. Enig and Innis even had a personal savings account. And they still kept emergency funds in the safe with the chest.

One evening as they were sitting on the porch in the cold air, Enig said, "Boy, am I glad I don't have to make anymore trips to Boston carrying secret documents."

"Did you ever learn what the documents were?"

"No, and I can't even begin to guess. You know, sweetheart, for the first time in our lives, we are free of British domination."

* * *

One day, quite by surprise, the *Venture* arrived at the Belfast port with cargo to unload from South Carolina and then she filled her holds with lumber from Hall's mill and two long masts.

Enig and Capt. McFee had a grand time with mugs of beer, talking about the war. "So where are you bound for from here, Hew?"

"This load of lumber and mast must go to Liverpool, then up to Greenock and take on tools made in the foundry there, then to New York. It's a great new world out there on the ocean now, Enig, without having to hide or chase English man-of-war ships.

"It looks like your boat business has really increased since the war."

"It has, and my son runs most of it. I'm proud of him."

"Oh, I almost forgot. The company that bought your business in Greenock, they went bankrupt before the war even started.

"I'll make some inquiries and see if maybe you might be able to ship a few of your boats to England. You still have the name and reputation. Except it is now a United States business."

Six weeks later, the *Venture* returned to Belfast and Hew asked Enig, "I can take two boats back with me to Liverpool. How fast can you have two built and crated for shipping? I'll be back here in a month. Can you have two ready by then?"

"Yes," no hesitation.

Enig hired four more workers and made sure those would be ready. The crew agreed to work weekends. The company now employed twelve men and a bookkeeper, who was also responsible to make sure the shop had all the building supplies needed. While Fergus and Lain were in charge of building boats to fill orders, Enig took charge of the two special orders for Liverpool.

Two days before the end of the deadline, Enig had the two boats crated and sitting on the dock. And right on schedule, the *Venture* returned, and after loading sawn lumber from Hall's mill, the two boats were loaded on deck and secured.

Hew paid him $150.00 for each boat. Enig had no idea how much he was selling them for. But Enig and Fergus were both satisfied with that price.

Within a year, Captain McFee was shipping four boats to Liverpool each trip, and he had also found a market in New Haven, Connecticut.

By 1790, the McFarney Boat Building Company was the largest employer in Belfast with thirty men. This also increased work at Hall's Mill and for Craig Randall's blacksmith shop. The town was prospering.

Enig and Innis were both fifty-four years old now. Fergus married a local girl, Debr,a in 1786. She was three years younger than him, and their first child was a boy they named Angus, meaning unique choice. Fergus' wife, Debra, chose the name. Fergus and Enig had by now built an addition onto the family home and Innis was glorified beyond belief. She had another woman's company and a grandson to help to take care of.

* * *

At the turn of the century, both Enig and Innis were now sixty-four years old. At Innis' insistence, Enig had finally given Fergus total responsibility for the boat building company. He was still a stalwart, rugged man, but he also knew he no longer had the stamina that he once had.

Fergus and family still lived at the original home, and Angus was now twelve years old and the shining star in his grandfather's eyes. The two would spend hours exploring the property, hunting, fishing and Angus learned how to fish for lobster like his dad did. Several times each summer the family would have steamed clams and lobsters cooked in seaweed over an open fire.

Sometimes in the evenings, Enig would tell his grandson stories about the old country and he would teach him how to speak using the old Scottish brogue dialect. And sometimes in school Angus would answer the teacher in the brogue dialect. Which usually got his ears or the end of his nose snapped.

Angus would ask his dad to tell him stories when he was fighting the British, but most often Fergus chose not to remember the fighting and killing and the senseless waste of human lives.

Fergus' wife, Debra, was now working full time in the company's office. When Angus was in school, Enig and Innis were once again alone on the homestead during the day.

They only had the one mule now, with two nanny goats for their milk, which Innis turned the cream into butter. Enig and Angus had also built a hen house and now the laying hens were well supplying the family with eggs.

There wasn't a weed in the whole garden. Everyday Enig would be on his hands and knees pulling weeds. He missed the shop, but at the same time he was enjoying these golden years. And Innis was just as happy watching her husband enjoying life.

One day as Enig and Innis were enjoying a cup of coffee on the porch, Innis asked, "What are we going to do with the chest?"

"I've been thinking about that lately. I think we'll have to leave it to Fergus with a few instructions.

"Tomorrow I'll go into town and talk with attorney Bill

Sylvester and have him draw up something that'll be binding.

Enig walked to town the next morning with Fergus and Debra. "Are you planning on working in the shop today, Dad?"

"No, I'm going to talk with an attorney, Bill Sylvester. Your mother and I decided it was time we have a will drawn up."

It was still too early to find Sylvester in his office, so Enig walked through the shop, marveling at all of the changes since the days in Greenock. Everyone there knew who Enig was and he spoke to each one as he walked by.

Finally in the attorney's office, Mr. Sylvester asked, "What can I do for you this morning, Enig? Another expansion of your boat factory?"

"No, I think it is time I make a will."

"I think that would be a very good idea, considering your business and all."

"Everything I say must be held in the strictest of confidence, at all times, Mr. Sylvester."

"Certainly. That goes without question."

"Our daughter, Blair Hagan, in Bangor, is to receive $10,000.00.

"The boat building business will become the property of our son, Fergus; and all proceeds of the company.

"Our house and land will also go to our son Fergus. With the stipulation that the property is never to be sold or lumbered or mined." This raised Sylvester's eyebrows but he didn't say anything. "And this stipulation must be passed down to each future generation. And this stipulation must be obeyed by each future generation under the penalty of law," Again Sylvester's eyebrows went up.

"Continue, Mr. McFarney."

"In our safe is a chest containing a document. And no one other than the beholder will know about it.

"And this chest and document must be willed in future generations to the beholder's son. No exceptions."

"Question, Mr. McFarney. It sounds as if you do not want any of your future generations to do anything with this document. Whatever it is."

"That's not quite the point. I'm fumbling for words here. I'll try without revealing too much. No one would be able to read this document. Perhaps in the future when science has developed, then whoever has the document then will know what to do with it."

"Where did this document come from Mr. McFarney? Can you tell me this?"

"No."

"Is it something that would be considered illegal to possess by the courts?"

"No."

"There is one more point. When it becomes necessary to execute this will, our daughter is not to know anything about the chest or document. As it is now, neither of our two children know anything about either one."

"Okay, who do you want as your executor?"

"The logical person would be yourself, Mr. Sylvester."

"Certainly."

"Now, when you have this written up, before it is signed, I want to take it home and let my wife read it. If she agrees, then we'll both sign it. And I will need your signature also, Mr. Sylvester."

"That goes without question.

"I would like to ask a question about this document."

"Go ahead; I may refuse to answer."

"You seem to think this document is important."

"I do."

"Does it have anything to do with the United States?"

"No—I don't know for sure."

"I can have this written up for you by the close of day. If you could pick it up tomorrow?"

"That'll be good. Maybe my wife will come in with me and we both can read it here."

He was home in time for lunch with Innis and while they ate, he told her about the will. "You'll have to go in tomorrow with me and we both will have to read it and if there aren't any changes, we both sign, and Sylvester signs it."

The will might have seemed a little lopsided towards Fergus, but because of the document, she understood.

They lay awake for a long time that night talking about the past. "Enig, what do you suppose that document is all about?"

"I wish I knew. I've tried not to think about it through the years, but there were times when it just wasn't possible."

"Me, too. Give me your best guess, sweetheart."

"A treasure—not so much a map, but more like directions where to find it."

"What kind of a treasure, sweetheart? Gold, jewels, silver or information? How long do you think it has been under the rock?" she asked.

"For a very, very long time. The soil around the rock was undisturbed. There was grass, weeds and bushes growing around the rock. I honestly believe it was put under the rock before this land was settled."

"Do you think whoever put it under the rock ever had intensions of returning to get it?"

"I really don't know. I suppose that would depend what the document had to say," he said.

"I suppose if whoever intended to return for it at some time would have left something on shore, a key maybe, where to look for the kidney shaped rock with a small dimple in the center. They would have to have had left something on shore for a beacon," Innis said.

Enig picked up on her thinking then, "And we have never found that beacon or clue that would say here, here is the kidney rock. So I don't think whoever put it there ever had any intention of returning for it."

She continued on this line of thinking, too. "Then we were meant to find it. I don't believe in coincidences. Look at the facts, sweetheart, before we came here. Your dad wanted you to join the Scottish Navy where you met Lieutenant Hew McFee and you two became friends. You both leave the navy and Hew purchases this huge parcel of land and when he learns you want to move to the new world, he sells you this land. We eventually cross the Atlantic and build here and we find the chest and document under the rock. All of these events were only gears in the turn of life. I honestly don't believe we just happened to build here; we have been guided here all along," Innis said.

They both were silent for a few moments thinking about what Innis had just said.

"So I think what you're saying, Innis, is that we were meant to discover it?"

"Well, what do you think?" she asked.

"I don't think that we just happened to find it. But who or what was guiding us?"

"I can't answer that, sweetheart, but look at this: you spent three years sailing for the Scottish Navy and you never had a close call to your life. We all crossed the ocean and again, there wasn't one single thing that was threatening to us. You made several trips to Boston and back carrying dispatches for the Continental Army and Fergus spent years in the Belfast Militia, and there were times when I was here alone with a young daughter. Not once were any of us in real danger. Yes, I think there is something greater than us that has been watching over us.

"But what, I do not understand," she continued, "if we were guided here to find the document—well, we'll never know what it says. So I have to ask, WHY?"

"Maybe our family has been chosen to protect its existence until sometime in the future when our descendants will be able to read and understand it."

"Then we must protect it with our lives, sweetheart," Innis said. Then she added—which puzzled him—"You know, this all started with your father when he wanted you to join the Scottish Navy where you met Hew McFee. Didn't Eachann sail for three years and didn't he travel to the new world? Who's to say he didn't put the chest and document under the rock?"

"Do you know what you are saying, Innis?"

"Yes, If he did, then he would also have to have been responsible for everything that brought us here; including discovering the document."

"Then he would have to have been more than consciousness. That's a powerful thought, Innis."

"Why do you suppose we were chosen?" Innis asked.

"I don't know, unless it's because we are who we are."

"You know, sweetheart, when I leave this physical world, I'll have one big regret."

"I think I know what that is, sweetheart. I too will regret not ever knowing what that document says or what it has to do with us."

"Maybe ... just maybe we might be able to reincarnate in the future when we will be able to understand what the document has to say," Enig said.

Innis squeezed his hand and said, "We will have to try."

* * *

The next morning, after Fergus and Debra had left for work, Enig and Innis walked Angus to school then they went to lawyer Sylvester's office.

"Good morning, Innis, I seldom see you in town now."

They both sat down in chairs and Sylvester handed them each a copy to read. Innis said, "Everything you have here I like, but I would like you to add that when we die our bodies should be buried next to the rock. One on each side. This way it'll prevent anyone from moving it."

"Good point, Innis," Enig said.

"And you, Enig?"

"I don't see anything in here that would prevent you from ever disclosing knowledge of the rock."

"Anything anyone says to their attorney is confidential and cannot be revealed to anyone."

"That's all fair and good, Mr. Sylvester, but I would like something added to this that you will not ever disclose the secrets the rock holds upon fear of being shot."

Innis looked strangely at her husband, surprised he would say something like that. So too was Attorney Bill Sylvester.

"I can add that also, Mr. McFarney, but in different language."

At the end of the will he added two codicils explaining their wishes. Enig's was toned down slightly.

All three signed all the papers of both copies and dated them. One copy would remain with Attorney Sylvester and the other went home with them.

"Sometime we are going to have to talk with Fergus, you know," Innis said. "Tomorrow is Saturday. I'll make some excuse and take Debra and Angus into town with me. This will give you a chance to talk with him."

* * *

After Innis left with Debra and Angus, Enig said, "Son, come into the living room. We need to talk. Sit down."

"Your mother and I had our will made out yesterday in Sylvester's office. The only way to get into this is let you read through it. Then we'll talk about it," and he gave him the copy.

When he had finished reading there was a strange expression on his face. "Before you say anything, son, open the safe and check it out," and he gave Fergus a slip of paper with the safe's combination. "Open it, son, and take it out."

Fergus still could not find anything to say, but he opened the safe and took the crest out and sat back in his chair with the chest in his lap. He only looked at his dad.

143

"Go ahead, son, open it." He waited.

He opened the chest and took out the document scroll.

"Unroll it and look at it, son."

He did and said, "I can't make anything out from this. What does it say? This isn't paper. What is it? And this chest isn't wood. What is it?"

"Your mother and I have kept this secret for thirty years. We both believe whatever is written must be very important."

Then he told his son everything that he and Innis had been talking about and explaining every detail of the rock and chest. "I understand now why you and Mom want to be buried on either side of the rock. That way no one will ever move it."

"During the war, son, your mother and I reburied it under the rock in case the British were able to overrun us. We didn't want it to fall into their hands. So in the future, if the need arises that is a safe place to hide it. Now you must keep this secret until you are ready to pass this on to Angus and he to his son and so forth."

"I understand, Dad."

"Sometime in a future generation, science will have advanced enough to discover what is said on the document. Until then, our family has been charged with its repository and secret.

"Memorize this combination and don't tell anyone until the time is right. You will be keeping a tremendous secret from your wife, but it must be this way."

"I understand, Dad; you can count on me."

"I don't think there is anything else I can tell you, so perhaps you'd better put it back in the safe."

When the three returned home, Enig and Fergus were sitting on the porch drinking coffee.

That night when they were alone, Innis asked, "How did it go with Fergus?"

"He was confused at first, but he slowly began to understand the secrecy involved.

"Now that we have our will made and the secret given to Fergus, if I leave this world tonight, I will feel better about the whole rock secret," Enig said.

Innis hugged and kissed him and they both went to sleep.

CHAPTER 15

In April of 1812, Enig died and a week later Innis died of a broken heart and loneliness. Fergus buried both his mom and dad on either side of the kidney rock and placed a marble memorial in front of the rock between the graves.

Blair had no problem that her brother Fergus had received the bulk of the inheritance. She was happy with her share and returned to Bangor.

With the passing of his father, Fergus suddenly realized he was now charged with the safety of the chest and document. Great Britain was stopping American merchant vessels and impressing the crews into British service aboard their ships and stealing the cargo and sinking the ships. Plus Great Britain was organizing the western and Central American Indian tribes to attack and stop the American westward movement.

Already Congress was calling for war and Fergus remembered what Enig had said. He withdrew $20,000.00 from his personal and business accounts and put that with the chest under the kidney rock. He buried more money in the root cellar and under the barn.

He was still building boats but the orders had slowed so much because of the British impressment he had to lay off all but eight men.

The company was still solvent with $20,000.00 in the bank. Fergus had managed to hide away over $60,000.00 total.

When his son Angus had turned eighteen in 1806, Fergus

talked with him about enlisting in the United States Navy. In 1807, he was nineteen and he had enlisted for four years. And because of his skills with building and repairing boats, in two years he was promoted to Bosun mate. And the executive commander was Lt. Hew McFee II, and he and Angus hit if off right away. Like their dads had.

On June 18 that year the United States had had enough of Great Britain's high handed tactics and impressment of American sailors on the open sea and declared war on Great Britain.

Many of the young men in the Belfast area had been called up for military duty. Everyday Fergus would walk into the general store for the newspaper looking for information of the war and any mention of his son's ship, *The Boston Tiger*. She had been in a few battles and had been the victor with only a few casualties.

Many communities in the Northeast, in particular the Maine territory of Massachusetts, had trade and business interests in Great Britain and there wasn't full support for the war. Fergus could remember when his family crossed the ocean to escape England's control and every facet of their lives. And although up until 1810 he had done a lot of business with companies in England, buying the McFarney-built fishing boats, he fully supported his country against the Commonwealth of England. His son, Angus, was on one of the United Sates battleships.

People in Belfast, although they may not have supported the United States' declaration of war, did support Angus and did not chastise the McFarneys.

Angus' four year enlistment was up the winter of 1813 and he volunteered to stay with the ship until the war was over or the ship was sunk. His father was proud of his son's decision to see the war through to the end.

By this time, in the summer of 1814, things were heating up in many of the coastal towns. Word came down from Castine that the British Royal Navy was making plans to attack Eastport first, then Castine, Machias, Bangor and Hampden.

This news did little to upset many in Belfast, but Fergus closed his business and boarded up the doors and windows and withdrew all of the company's funds from the bank. He gave each employee $100.00 in hopes they would return to work when the war was over.

He took those funds and the cache he had in the shop and put everything in another chest under the kidney rock. "All we can do, Debra, is hope for the best."

"Oh I hope so, Fergus. This news scares me."

"Me, too, sweetheart."

From the book *A Quandry at Knowles Corner:*

The news of the impending attacks by British forces went inland a hundred and fifty miles north of Bucksport to two Hastings families who had started trapping and farming a mile and a half north of Knowles Corner on the Aroostook Trail.

Two brothers, Bill and Gus Hastings, were fishermen in Bucksport and one day on a trip on rough ocean water, they had to seek shelter out of a storm on an isolated island, the Grandmanan Island, where they witnessed the burial of a treasure chest and the captain shooting the two men who helped him with the burial of the chest.

When Captain Holigard left they stole the chest and moved their families and their father to T7-R5 in the country.

Now fearing if the British were to regain control of Castine and Maine, they joined the army to fight in Castine. They left their father there in T7-R5 with the two families. They thought the families would be okay with their father and their sons to protect them.

It was a short battle for Castine and the British defeated the volunteers and the two Hasting brothers were killed. The British renamed the town, New Ireland.

But the occupation only lasted eight months. Negotiations

to end the war were already being discussed in February of 1815 and the fighting, or most of it, stopped. Then in September of 1815, in the Treaty of Ghent, the war was officially over and all of the British forces left the United States.

Before the siege of 1814, Maine, still a territory of Massachusetts, representatives from Maine pleaded with Massachusetts for support which never came.

This failure to support Maine didn't go over well with much of the citizens of Maine, and in 1816 a vote to separate from Massachusetts failed to pass. Another vote in July 26, 1819, did pass and in 1820 Maine became a separate state.

* * *

Angus was discharged from duty in the United States Navy in April of 1814 and returned home. He wanted to open the shop and go back to building boats. But Fergus said, "Not yet, son. The treaty hasn't been ratified yet and even when it is, it'll take time for people and businesses to get over the effects of the war."

"Then what do we do, Dad?"

"We fish until it's time to build boats."

"And when will that be?"

"We'll know when the time is right." A little of his dad and grandad was showing in his character.

* * *

Fergus and his son, Angus, went out every other day fishing; weather permitting. Robert and Helen Kilgore had purchased the general store years ago from the Cummins and they agreed to take every fish the McFarneys caught.

Life was slowly returning to normal, what it had been before the war. But the boat business didn't start until the summer of 1820 when a tall mast ship arrived and needed repairs.

With help from the merchant crew, they were eight days repairing two tall masts. When they had finished, Angus said, "Dad, I want to reopen the shop."

Fergus didn't argue, he had enjoyed work on the *Sea Princess* out of Savannah, Georgia. "Okay, It's time."

Fergus redeposited $20,000.00 in the company's bank account and hired two men until business picked up. Debra wrote up an advertisement that the McFarney Boat Company was back in business and she mailed the advertisement to the newspapers in Boston and New York.

Before they had their first boat off the ways, orders started coming in and Fergus soon had to hire twelve more men. "Your advertisements, sweetheart, put us back in business," Fergus said.

The oversea business had not started yet, and that was okay with Fergus, as they were still getting back up to snuff. There were sufficient orders coming in from south of New England.

In the summer a new teacher took over the Belfast school, an April Hume from Bangor and graduate of a teaching normal school. She was twenty-eight years old and single. She needed a summer job and stopped at the boat shop and Debra hired her on the spot to help with the bookkeeping.

The first time Angus and April met their eyes locked onto each other. And then Angus smiled and broke the ice. They were married that summer before school started and they lived at the McFarney home.

* * *

Soon after the turn of the New Year, so many orders were coming in, the shop was back to its full complement of thirty men.

Fergus and Debra now were each sixty-three years old and like his dad, he left the heavy work to the crew. He maintained more or less a supervisory position.

In July of that year, April gave birth to a son they named Owen Fergus McFarney. Two years later a girl was born; they named her Barbara. And, like his folks and grandparents, Fergus and Debra were enjoying their grandchildren. As soon as they could walk they would take them for walks along the sandy shore and show 'em how to dig for clams.

When Owen was older, Fergus would take him in the fishing boat after haddock for the family.

One day as Fergus was sitting on the porch by himself, he began thinking about the McFarney family. He had never seen any bickering between his parents, Enig and Innis. He never knew his great grandparents, but from listening to stories from his parents, he had formed a very good opinion of them both.

His grandfather had gone to sea. His father had run dispatches alone between Belfast and Boston. His dad had joined the Belfast militia and served three years securing the safety of the surrounding towns. And Angus had spent four years in the Navy fighting the British again. *And not one of us has ever been wounded. Almost as if someone is looking after the family.*

Then he started thinking about the hidden chest and document inside. How was his family tied into whatever was written on it?

In 1828, he and his wife, Debra, turned seventy years old and he knew it was time to tell his son Angus about the chest and document. So on one weekend while Debra and April had gone to town with Owen and Barbara, Fergus took his son into his confidence and told him all about the chest and document.

Angus looked at the document, but he, like his dad and grandad, was not able to make any sense from it. And he understood the importance of keeping it a secret, even from the rest of the family. "Maybe sometime, Dad, science will have evolved enough so one of our descendants will be able to decipher this. I understand the stipulations grandad put down and I'll guarantee they will be upheld and the secret protected."

"And mother does not know about any of this?"

"That's right, son. I didn't like keeping the secret from her, but I never felt as if I had any choice."

"Okay, Dad, I will continue the secrecy."

"My advice, son, put it in the safe and forget about it, until it is time to pass it on to your son, Owen. Because if you don't, It'll drive you crazy thinking about it."

Angus nodded his head.

During the next two days, all Angus could think about was the chest and document. *Who had written it? Who buried it under the kidney rock? And what did it say?* But work at the shop brought him back to reality. April had noticed how quiet Angus had become during those two days. And when she asked about it, all he would say was work at the shop.

One evening at the supper table, Angus said, "Orders are coming in so fast now, Dad, we're six months behind. If we hire any more men we'll have to enlarge the shop again."

"Well, there's certainly enough room to enlarge. But before we do, let's try something else first," Fergus said.

"What do you have in mind?"

"Well, as it is now one crew starts a new boat and sees it through to completion. What if we had a crew that only made the ribs. They could certainly stay ahead of the assembly crew. Another crew cutting the pieces, another crew doing all the steaming and bending and maybe only two or three crews assembling the pieces. When one cutting crew had enough pieces or parts made up ahead of the assembly crew, then they could start work on another boat until more parts were needed."

"I think you have something there, Dad. Why don't you come to work with me tomorrow and we'll see about laying out areas to do this. Create an assembly line. I really like the idea, Dad."

* * *

The next day, they both saw areas where they could make changes and after a week of reorganizing, they began the assembling process. Fergus was so excited he made a point to be in the shop to see how well the system functioned.

After six months their production had increased thirty percent and orders were no longer being turned down.

In the late winter of 1830, Fergus began to feel his body slowing down to the point where he no longer could walk the half mile to the shop or do any physical work or heavy lifting.

He knew his time was short and he was also glad he had had the talk with his son about the chest and document. He now could pass on to the next level of existence with only one regret: not knowing what the document said.

On April 1st of 1830, Fergus didn't get up in the morning. He lay on his back with the blankets pulled up under his chin and his hands clasped on his stomach on the blankets. "My word, April, Mom, look, Dad died smiling."

He was buried with his folks in front of the kidney rock. "I will lay beside you soon, my husband," Debra said.

Owen felt as sad as anyone. His grandad had always been his friend and playmate.

Two years later on the same day, Debra left the physical world forever and she was buried beside her husband, Fergus.

* * *

In 1832, Owen was ten years old and his little sister, Barbara, was eight. And like their parents and grandparents before them, they dug clams everyday at low tide from which they earned a little money each week. His dad, Angus, was now forty-four, and he had the same build and disposition as his dad and grandad. Tall ships had not come in for some years now looking for repairs.

But the company was doing such a tremendous business, it didn't miss the tall sails repairs.

Owen was much like his dad, Angus, and at an early age he had explored most of the half-mile square of land. And he was the first McFarney to trap and enjoy hunting.

Moose were still being seen in the cranberry marsh, and each fall he would shoot a bull, and then work two days bringing all the meat back to the house.

The Kilgore General Store bought his fur, and like his

granddads before him, he saved every penny.

At age eighteen in 1840, like his granddads, he enlisted in the United States Navy and saw much of the world. He liked sailing and navy life. But he knew he had to carry on the McFarney boat business.

In 1865 war broke out between the states and although the company never had to close its doors, business had slowed. And they were back repairing tall mast ships for the Union Navy. Enough young men had either enlisted or were drafted, so the company never had to let any worker go.

By now, Owen had married Bridget Smith and they had two sons, Bryce in 1850 and Thomas in 1852. Angus would take the two boys out sailing and at an early age he was letting them each sail the boat. Only if he was with them, though. The two boys also discovered they could catch lobsters in front of their house using a fish pole baited with clams, like their great grandfather Fergus did. And once again the family would enjoy an occasional steamed clams and lobster cookout.

When the war ended, the company began building boats again as fast as they could.

When Owen was seventy years old in 1892, he passed on the secret of the chest and document to his oldest son, Bryce. "Some time, son, one of our descendants will be able to decipher this and understand what is written. Until then, this must be kept a secret."

"I understand, Dad."

Through the years, Bryce felt guilty about keeping such an important secret from his family, in particular his wife, Ann. *But I gave my word to my dad years ago.*

His dad, Owen, passed away in the spring of 1900, and his mother, Barbara, passed in September of 1900.

Bryce checked the family record book and found it very peculiar that all, except one grandparent, had passed not long after the first one.

The McFarney Company was still stable and before the passing of Owen, he had suggested to his son, Bryce, that instead of wasting all of the scrap material, they should start building smaller boats. Dingies.

And before Owen's death, he saw this plan succeed. The dingy was selling as fast as the fishing boats.

After Owen's passing in April of 1900, Bryce contacted markets in Portland, Bangor and New Haven, Connecticut, and began shipping six fishing boats and four dingies once a month on the Maine Central Railroad. MCR had a branch line that terminated in Belfast.

The Hall sawmill was also doing a great business. Of course since Cameron Hall, the mill had had several different owners. It was now operated by Eric Clifton and he had upgraded the mill to a bandsaw and new planers.

Bryce's brother, Thomas, didn't want anything to do with the family business and when he was twenty-five in 1877, his father, Owen, gave him a lump sum of money and he boarded the train for California and no one had heard from him again.

Bryce and Ann had two girls first, and then a son. "There, Bryce, you have your son, no more babies," Ann had said. The son was named Delbert after Ann's father. Owen lived long enough to see his grandson and told him many stories of his many great grandparents.

"When I finish school, Granddad, I want to go in the navy," Del said.

"You'd make me proud, Del," his granddad had said.

Del was eight years old when his grandparents passed away, and not to sure what passing away was all about. He only knew he missed his grandparents, his granddad in particular.

* * *

Del turned eighteen in 1910 and he also finished school. He took the train to Bangor and talked with a navy recruiter. He signed up for four years.

He would have to leave home on July 1st. Because of his carpentry experience, he was assigned to the carpentry shop and reassigned to a US Navy base in England, near Liverpool. He was surprised how big the Atlantic Ocean was. He had never stopped to think about it before.

He spent two years onshore in the carpentry shop before receiving a new assignment aboard a destroyer, the *Jefferson*.

At the end of his enlistment, he had seen all he wanted of the world outside of Belfast, Maine. He had met a few people he would call friend, but many of them were stuck on themselves. No, it was time to go home.

He was discharged only thirty days before fighting erupted in Europe, when on June 28, 1914, Garrilo Princip, a Bosnian Serb Yugoslav nationalist member of Serbian Black Hand military society assassinated the Astro-Hungarian heir, Archduke Franz Ferdinand. Within a month of the assassination, Europe was divided into two factions, eventually affecting the entire world.

Bryce met his son, Delbert, at the train depot when he arrived home. "Son, am I glad you didn't get pulled into the fighting in Europe. This is going to be a bad one."

When Del walked through the door at home, his mother, Ann, collapsed in his arms, crying. She was so glad to see her son home.

Bryce and Ann both turned sixty-four that spring and like his forefathers before him, he still went to work each day. But— of course there were days when he would return home early.

Del went right to work in the boat shop, with a much different attitude. He had filled out and put on weight in the four years and his mental attitude was much sharper now. He soon learned to do everyone's job in the shop, and even though Tom Beedy was the shop foreman, Del soon became the company's supervisor.

When Bryce turned sixty-five, he turned running the boat

shop over to Del, and Bryce and Ann began to enjoy themselves now that each had more time.

On a business trip to Rockland one day, Del met the love of his life, Rebecca Cortland, and they were soon married.

The following year Rebecca gave birth to a girl, Belle. Ann was so happy to have a little girl in the house now, and much to her surprise, Bryce really enjoyed his little granddaughter.

The time was coming close when Bryce knew he had to pass on the secret to his son, Delbert. So one Sunday in 1920, while Ann, Rebecca and Belle were at church, Bryce called his son into the living room.

"Sit down, son, there is something I must pass on to you before I die," and he handed him a slip of paper with the combination to the safe. "Open it, son, and take it out."

"Take what out, Dad?"

"Open it and you'll see." This was getting mysterious. He opened it.

And of course the chest stood out over all the papers in the safe. He took it out and sat down with the chest in his lap. "It isn't very heavy."

"Open it, son."

He did and withdrew the scrolled document and just held it in his hands without speaking. "Unroll it, son, and look at it."

There were so many things going through his mind now. *What was he holding? Some foreign declaration? A treasure map? Orders to assassinate someone?*

After a few moments he unrolled the scroll and looked at it dumbfounded. "What is this, Dad? I can't read it."

"Neither can I, nor any of our forefathers before us, son."

Then he told his son everything he could about the chest and document and how it became a part of the McFarney family.

He was sworn to secrecy as were the many forefathers before him. "Some day, son, one of our descendants, with new advancements in science, will be able to read and understand this."

"There is no idea who might have buried it under the kidney rock to begin with?"

"Not unless it is in that document."

"I understand now why this must be kept a secret. I can assure you, Dad, that I will protect the chest, document and the secret. I only hope I live long enough to find out what it says."

"I can assure you, son, all of us have wished for the same."

* * *

Six years after Belle was born, in 1922, Rebecca gave birth to a son, Myles.

The war in Europe had ended four years ago and worldwide, the prosperity was good. People had money and were willing to spend it. Old customers were buying new boats and Del talked with his dad about a new idea. "Dad, people have money and they aren't afraid to spend it. I would like to start building a new type of boat."

"What do you have in mind Son?"

"A forty-foot pleasure boat. A yacht. I've drawn up some plans," and he handed them to his dad.

Bryce took several minutes to look them over and finally said, "Okay, let's try one. Keep good records of cost."

Before they could start building the first yacht, they had to build onto the factory building. But during that time, Del started forming the ribs, spars, hull and keel, so once work could begin, parts would be ready.

It was slow going at first with the prototype, but a year after Bryce had given his approval, the yacht was rolled off the ways into the harbor. There was only one sail and a six cylinder gasoline engine which turned a propeller, and during the trial run the yacht could maintain thirty miles an hour.

People from all along the Maine coast were coming to see this yacht and the first week after the trials, the company took orders for six. The yacht was such a success, Del gave the employees a Christmas bonus plus a pay raise.

Bryce's wife, Ann, died in 1928 at age seventy-eight, and for two years Bryce moped around the house. His only interest was with his grandson, Myles.

One day sitting on the porch watching the clouds he was thinking how much the boat building industry had expanded. It was beyond his understanding now. Then he began thinking of his great grandfathers and their ingenuity to build such a profitable business. He wished he could go back in time and visit all of his great grandfathers.

He was serenely happy since his wife left him alone two years earlier. With a smile on his face, he suddenly found his physical body would sleep now forever.

His wife, Ann, greeted him to the Astral World, and behind her were his long list of great grandparents that he had wished to visit.

That same year, 1950, Rebecca gave birth to another son, Egan.

CHAPTER 16

The new yacht was very popular with the boating world and those who could afford them. The McFarney Boat Company was now building three a year and the profit margin with these three pieces was almost equal to that of the fishing boat total.

In 1940, Myles turned eighteen, and because of another war in Europe, he chose the Army Air Force instead of the Navy. And he chose to be a fighter pilot.

After his training was complete, he was sent to England.

Tragedy hit the McFarney family in 1942, when they received word that their son Myles had been shot down over the English Channel.

When the United States became totally involved with this new war in Europe, the boat building business slowed but they didn't have to close the shop. They were only building one yacht each year and the number of fishing boats and dingies were fewer. They were able to stay in business.

During this time, Del looked into a new material to use on both the yachts and fishing boats. He had been in touch with Owens-Corning chemical company. They had developed a polyester resin, fiberglass. It was used as a coating or covering over the wooden hull. The finished product was stronger and sleek looking which caught the attention of boat owners.

In the spring of 1945, Del didn't know why, but he thought it was important now to tell his only son, Egan, about the chest and document. He waited until he and Egan were alone. Then he opened the safe and removed the chest and gave it to Egan.

Egan was surprised and shocked that this had been kept a secret from the family all through seven generations and no one ever suspected.

When Del had finished, Egan promised to continue the secret. "Maybe sometime soon, Dad, we'll be able to discover what this says. Science is advancing fast now."

"I hope so, son."

That summer of 1945, after Japan had surrendered unconditionally, Delbert suddenly died of a massive heart attack at the shop. The whole town was devastated, in particular the McFarney Boat Company and family. Egan was only fifteen and he was ready to quit school and take over the company. But his mother, Rebecca, put her foot down and said, "I appreciate what you want to do, son, but there is no way I am going to let you quit school. And I think your father would have agreed with me. No Egan, you stay in school. We'll work something out."

Their second child, Belle, was married and living out of state with her own family. So running the company fell to Rebecca.

The shop foreman, Bruce Harvey, was doing a great job and she left him where he was. The accountant had all she could do, so she decided to hire a company manager.

She placed an advertisement in the newspaper and had several interviews. She was particularly interested in Harold Bean. He had worked on one of the assembly lines when he was in high school, so he was familiar with the building process. After high school he had gone to college for business.

Rebecca had made up her mind with Mr. Bean. "You'll oversee the shop, Mr. Bean, but unless you have something constructive to say about its operations, I want most of the shop managing left to the foreman, Phillip Russell. He has been with the company for fifteen years and has always done a good job.

"You are to oversee the company's financial end. That

includes new and old customers, material acquisitions. Do you have any problem with this, Mr. Bean?"

"No, none at all."

"Good, our accountant, Nancy Herbert, will be invaluable to you."

Until Harold Been was well situated in the company and his position as company manager, Rebecca would spend a half a day there helping him to get started.

The company really was affected by the passing of Del. Everyone liked him and thought of him more as a friend than an employer and boss. But after a year adjusting to the new manager and the end of WWII, the company's profits started increasing.

Meanwhile, Egan spent all of his free time in the shop, learning the business.

In 1948 Egan turned eighteen and it was always his dream to join the navy and see the world. That all changed when his father died. With the responsibility of the secret, Egan knew he could not go trapsing around the world.

Shortly after Egan had graduated from high school, a family moved to Belfast from Allagash. Kelly McBride came to the McFarney Company looking for a job.

"Allagash to Belfast is a great distance, Mr. McBride."

"250 miles."

"What brought you to Belfast?"

"I wanted more for my children than just woods."

"What brought you here to this shop? What kind of work have you been doing?"

"I am a carpenter by trade. I can do some electrical wiring and plumbing, although I'm not licensed to do either. Even in Allagash, I read about your boat business."

"How big is your family?"

"My wife and me; we have six children. Three years ago my wife's sister and husband were killed in an automobile accident and their only child, a girl, Alison, now lives with us.

Alison finished school this year and she is the oldest of the seven children."

"What is Alison's last name?"

"Jackson."

"Let's go for a walk around the shop, Mr. McBride."

Egan walked him through the entire shop and introduced him to the shop's foreman.

At the end of the tour, Egan asked, "Did you see anything that interested you, Mr. McBride?"

"I like working with wood. Either on the wood framework or finishing the interior with wood."

"When can you start, Mr. McBride?"

"Please, call me Kelly. Mr. sounds so formal. I can start tomorrow morning."

Kelly left and Egan went back to work.

A week after Kelly started work, Egan asked the foreman how Kelly was doing. "I started him on the framework then three days later one of the finish guys couldn't make it to work because of sickness and I asked Kelly to fill in. He is an artist with finish work. I think I'll keep him there for now."

"Thanks, Robert."

One afternoon during the lunch period, Egan stopped at the drug store and when he stepped up to the checkout counter and saw the young woman there; he just stood there looking at her. She was looking straight back at him and just as tongue tied. It was like two friends meeting after a long separation.

"Excuse me for staring—I couldn't help myself. You're new here, aren't you?"

"Yes, my family has only recently relocated here in Belfast and this is my first week clerking here."

"Welcome to Belfast. My name is Egan McFarney."

"Oh, you own the boat factory. You hired my uncle recently."

"Yes, Kelly McBride, and you must be Alison."

163

More people were coming in and before leaving Egan said, "Maybe we could talk more over coffee."

"I would like that. I work 8 a.m. to 5 p.m.," she said.

They did meet for coffee two days later. "You seem awful young to be running a company as big as yours," Alison said.

"When my father died, I had no alternative. I had originally wanted to join the navy and see the world."

"Maybe that is not what you were supposed to do," she said.

"I never thought of it like that before."

They would meet for coffee and conversation twice a week for a month. And their conversations were getting serious. His mother, Rebecca, was happy her son had found someone. An interest outside of the company.

They were soon married and Rebecca now had female companionship at home.

Ten months later, Alison gave birth to a daughter. Rebecca was ecstatic now, having a baby girl to help raise.

The next year Alison gave birth to a son, Edward. The following year another son, Paul. By now Egan decided he had to build on an addition to the house. He drew up some plans and asked Alison's dad, Kelly, "Kelly, I'm going to pull you out of the boat shop for awhile. I would like you to build this new addition onto my house," and he gave the plans to him.

"We need another bedroom and a full indoor bathroom. I'll hire some local boys to help you."

The new addition was complete by the end of summer, the full bathroom and all. "I'm so glad we don't have to use the outhouse any more, son," Rebecca said.

Egan also installed a floor-mounted oil furnace. The first time the old homestead had central heating.

Alison was a great mother and she cherished her three growing children, as did her husband and Rebecca.

Orders for the new yachts were coming in faster than ever

now and Egan had to make a decision. In order to make room for more yachts to be built, he had to eliminate half of the fishing boat berths. There was now room for the building for three yachts and four berths for fishing boats.

The McFarney Boat Building Company was such a nice place to work, the only employees who ever left were the young men going into the military. Egan paid his men better wages than they could expect anywhere in the state and he now was giving each a $200.00 Christmas bonus.

He, like his father and grandfathers before him, enjoyed his children. At a young age he would take all three with him out in the fishing boats and teach them how to sail. Rachel, the oldest, enjoyed fishing for haddock more than she did sailing. But the two boys were natural sailors.

* * *

Rebecca lived long enough to see her third grandson, Enos, born in 1972, fifteen years after the birth of Paul. She was content and happy and she certainly missed her husband, Del. He had been a good husband and father.

At the birth of Enos, Egan and Alison had turned forty-two years old. From an early age, Enos was proving to be an explorer. Always getting into things and mischief. His curiosity didn't go unnoticed by Egan.

Five years later in 1977, Rebecca quietly died one day as she was sitting on the porch shelling peas. And she, like many of the McFarneys before her, passed with a smile on her face.

* * *

In 1977, both Edward and Paul were drafted into the army and after basic training they both were sent to Germany. "At least they are together over there, Egan. I hope they come home," Alison said.

With both boys gone, running the boat company once again was up to Egan. Enos would go in with his dad on Saturdays to help sweep the floors and pick up the wood scraps, but he had very little interest in the company, other than he wanted to help his dad.

Rachel was in college and pregnant and due to get married after the baby came.

At age seven, Enos started collecting rocks, mostly the shiny and odd shaped stones. He even had a tin can full of different colored sea glass.

When Enos was eight years old, he would take trips across the property exploring and looking for shiny rocks. By now the property lines were well painted and there was little worry of him getting lost.

When Edward and Paul returned home after their hitch in the army, they were anxious to get back to work in the company. The army life had changed them some, Egan observed. They began pushing employees to work faster. And they were money hungry. And instead of living at home, they each rented an apartment in town.

"Egan, Edward and Paul have changed so much it's as if I don't know them anymore," Alison said.

"I know. Something happened to them in the army. Maybe it'll work out of them. I hope."

The two boys didn't change and Egan found he had to keep a tight rein on both. The company was still doing a great business, but the employees were not as happy as they used to be.

Besides enjoying the outdoors exploring and his rock collection, Enos was also very studious. He loved reading history books and he had decided at an early age that he wanted to be a scientist.

This pleased his dad. *Maybe he will discover what the secret holds.*

* * *

In 1987, Edward and Paul wanted to stop building fishing

boats and dingies and concentrate on the luxury yachts. "Dad, we have to build a dozen fishing boats to equal the profit of one yacht. We can cut our work force down and in the end we'll make more money than we are now or have ever made," Edward said.

"I don't like the idea. This company was built on making fishing boats over two hundred years ago in Greenock, Scotland," Egan said.

"Dad, we have to go where the money is," Paul said.

"I don't like the idea, boys. But I'll do this, I'll think about it over the weekend and I'll give you my answer Monday morning," Egan said.

After supper that evening Alison asked, "Why are you so quiet, sweetheart? Are there problems at work?"

"Problems? Yeah, it's Edward and Paul."

"What about them?"

"They want to stop making the fishing and dingy boats and concentrate on the yachts."

"What's the problem?

"This company had its start over two hundred years ago in Greenock, Scotland, building fishing boats. I just hate to stop. It's become the McFarney trademark in the boat building industry. It's become the McFarney family logo. I just hate to change."

"Would it be so bad? I mean to change?"

"It's more than just that. Edward and Paul are money hungry and I think they would like me out of the company. Besides, Edward already said they would be able to lay off half of the men. And that's not what the McFarney Company is about. We have made good money and a lot of it. But we have always used our people good.

"We're fifty-seven years old now, Egan. Maybe it's time we retired."

"Our sons may be forcing me into retirement."

"What about Enos?"

"Well, I've been thinking on that also. He's too much like me to be able to get along with his two older brothers. They'd run ramshrod over him. I want him to go to college.

"I have the weekend to think on it. I don't have to make a decision until Monday morning."

"I'm going to Bangor in the morning and Rachel and I are going shopping. This will give you time to talk with Enos."

"You know, sweetheart, you always were the smart one. We'll go for a walk out back and look at the trees."

Egan came across a path he didn't know was there, "How did this path get here?"

"I made it, Dad."

"Well, let's follow it. You lead the way. I've always been so busy with the company I never had much time to come out here." The trees were huge, since no one was allowed to cut them according to Enig's original will. Thick moss carpeted the ground under the softwood trees. There were deer in the cranberry marsh. The moose had long ago moved further inland away from populated areas.

Egan realized he was seeing this forest as did the early McFarney settlers. He was glad Enig had stipulated in his will that the forest would never be lumbered.

Halfway through they came to a moss-covered bank and Egan said, "Let's sit down, son."

"Are you tired, Dad?"

"No, we need to talk."

"Okay, about what?"

"What do you want to do when you finish high school, son? Do you want to stay with the company like Edward and Paul?"

"I hope I don't hurt your feelings Dad, but no. I have other interests and besides, Edward and Paul are so much older than me I doubt if I would have much of any say in the company. Let the two of them have it and I'll go my own way."

168

That's what Egan wanted to hear and right then it had made up his mind what he was going to do. "What do you want, son?"

"I want to go to the university and study geology."

"That is a good field. You start high school this fall. To be a geologist you'll have to take all the math and science courses you can."

"I like both math and science. I have already signed up for both this year."

"I'm glad to hear that. Now back to the company. Monday morning I am giving the company to Edward and Paul and I will be out of it. I don't like the direction the two want the company to go.

"Now, down to you, Enos. Also on Monday I am signing the deed to this property and house over to you. The new deed will have a codicil clause stating that your mother and I will have lifetime occupancy. I will also set up a trust fund for you. Two actually. One when you graduate from high school and the other one when you graduate from college. I'm not going to tell you how much either one will contain. The second trust will be substantial, though. And this you need to keep from your brothers."

"Okay, Dad," that's all he could think to say.

* * *

That night while Egan and Alison were alone in their bedroom, he told her what he had decided to do. "Are you sure, Egan?"

"Yes, more so now that Enos and I talked. I think Edward and Paul would eventually force Enos and I both out of the company. I think this is the only way."

After the shop started working Monday morning, Egan called Edward and Paul to his office and told them what he had decided. "When I leave here, I'll go to our attorney and have him draw up the transfer papers.

"There is 2.3 million dollars in the company account and

today I'll transfer 2.2 million to your mother and my personal account. I give you the company, plus one hundred thousand dollars to get you started. That should be sufficient."

"We never expected you to leave the company, Dad," Edward said.

"This is the only way. Both of you are too money hungry and eventually you would force me out.

"There's something else also," and he told them he was deeding the property and house to Enos. Neither one objected.

They stood then and shook hands. "I'll let you know when the papers will be ready to sign," and he left the shop and walked to the Sylvester and Sylvester, Attorney at Law, office.

Two days later Egan and Alison met their two sons in Sylvester's office. They each had copies to read, no one objected, they signed the documents and the brothers left. Then Egan and Alison signed the house and property over to Enos. Attorney Sylvester kept a copy and handed Egan the original.

The funds had been transferred on Monday.

"Here is a check for Rachel the next time you drive up to visit."

"Wow, a hundred thousand dollars?"

"Yes, I also put that same amount in a trust fund for Enos when he graduates high school."

CHAPTER 17

Four years passed and after Enos' graduation, Egan and Alison gave him his trust fund. He had been accepted at the university in Orono and he was able to pay for college from his trust fund. He also bought a two year old Subaru Legacy car.

That summer he and his dad spent a lot of time fishing for haddock. And once a week Alison would drive to Bangor and spend the day with Rachel.

Enos was anxious to start college in September and when the day came to leave home, he said a happy goodbye. Not that he was leaving his home, but he was looking forward to his studies.

Egan traded his old Ford pickup for a new GMC 4x4 with an extended cab, red and silver, with a snowplow. "I have an idea, Egan, let's take a road trip to northern Maine and I'll show you where I grew up."

"Okay, let's wait for the fall foliage. I have never been north of Bangor," he said. "We'll need someone to house sit for us."

"That won't be a problem. I've been planning this trip for a few weeks, and do you remember Judy in Enos' class?"

"Yes."

"She is a waitress in the Belfast Café and she said she would house sit any time we wanted to go somewhere. And I told her while she is here she can use my car."

"Then all we have to do is wait for the foliage," he said.

* * *

They took I-95 north and were enjoying how bright the foliage was. They stopped in Medway for a late breakfast and while Alison was looking at the placemat, she saw an advertisement for Baxter State Park. "We ought to go there some time, Egan."

"Next year?"

They got back on I-95 and pulled into a scenic turnout overlooking Salmon Stream Lake and Mt. Katahdin. "This would be a nice place to build a house," Egan said.

Alison took several pictures and they each took one of the other leaning against the white wooden fence with Mt. Katahdin in the background.

They continued on with Alison studying the road map. "We can either get off the Sherman exit and hit Rt.11—that'll take us to Fort Kent—or we can go on to Oakfield and take Rt. 212 to Rt. 11 at Knowles Corner."

"Let's take the Sherman exit."

Just before reaching Patten, Rt. 11 followed the crown of hills and both sides were farmland and beautiful views. They stopped at another scenic turnout on top of the hill before entering town. Alison took more pictures.

"Look at all of this unsettled land. And except for those farm fields we just drove through, this is all wilderness woodland," Egan said.

They stopped for gas at Gallagher's gas station just before the town proper. "Small town," Egan observed.

"They'll get smaller, if I remember."

Five miles north of Patten, the woods closed in around them. "I'm glad we filled up with gas when we did."

For the next fifty miles, most of the vehicles on Rt. 11 were heavy log trucks and it didn't take a set of scales to see that most of them were overloaded. "I never dreamed there was so much wilderness," Egan said.

"I think I had forgotten just how much there is. It's been fifty years since I left Allagash."

The colors were remarkable, mixed in with the green conifer trees. Eagle Lake looked like a resort town, except it was situated in the middle of the wilderness.

They decided to find a motel in Fort Kent and make the trip to Allagash in the morning.

They found a restaurant next to the St. John River and were given a window seat. As they waited for their orders, Alison asked, "What's the matter, Egan? You have been so quiet all day. Would you had rather stayed home?"

"No, it isn't that. There's a couple of things actually. One, we have seen some very beautiful country and the foliage is so bright. I have spent my entire life in Belfast, never traveling beyond Bangor. I feel I have missed out on so much, after seeing all of this wilderness. I have never given it a second thought before now.

"And two; I don't know if you'll understand, cause it is difficult to put into words. When we stopped at the scenic turnout north of Medway, while we were looking at mountains and the wilderness country between us and the mountains—I could feel the vibrations of a time long ago. As if in my mind I was experiencing another life in that mountainous wilderness.

"It happened again at the scenic turnout in Patten. Again between Patten and Knowles Corner and again as we drove through Eagle Lake.

"I have never experienced anything like this before."

"Maybe in another life you were actually part of this wilderness and seeing it again now has awakened primal memories," Alison said trying to comfort him.

But that wasn't all that Egan had on his mind. For reasons he couldn't explain, he began worrying about the chest and the document held within. The secret would have to be passed on to his son Enos, but when? If he had the secret now, then that might interfere with his college studies. And for another unexplained reason, Egan knew it was important for Enos to be a geologist. Maybe he will be the one who can find the answers.

After supper they found a walking path along the river. After a mile they found a bench to sit on. "This is the biggest river I have ever seen," he said.

"Well, it isn't just one river. There's the St. Francis, the Little Black, the Big Black and Allagash River. The St. John and the Big Black, and the St. Francis all start in Quebec, Canada. When there's a lot of ice in the winter and then if there is a warm rain in the spring, the ice will break up and flow downstream and jam and the river will flood.

"You want to hear something funny?" she asked.

"What?"

"Most of the people in Allagash are from an Irish descent and most of them speak French."

"French speaking Irishmen. Isn't that a little strange?" he asked.

"The Irish came into the country from Quebec and New Brunswick. They started potato farming and they could use the St. John to get their potatoes down river to markets. A lot of the men took French girls for wives and they learned to speak French. Both of my parents were Irish and spoke French. My mother could also speak English and insisted that I learn English."

They found many homes, but not clustered together. They drove across the bridge to the Walker Brook Road. They didn't go far and Alison said, "Stop, this is where I lived with my folks. There was a log cabin in this clearing. Let's turn around, Egan. This is bringing back memories I thought I had forgotten. Let's go. I wish now we hadn't come out here."

"Where did your aunt and uncle live?"

"I'll show you. About a mile from this bridge. I'll show you."

"What did your father do for work?"

"He worked in the woods, before he started carpentry. There, that gray shingled house."

"That's a nice house."

"It was Uncle Kelly who built it."

From Allagash they followed Rt. 1 through the farm country close to the New Brunswick border and home.

* * *

During that first year in college, Enos tried to get home on weekends. It was always nice and relaxing to return home. His course study was rugged but he excelled. He was learning something new and he found it challenging.

In June, after college was out until fall, the McFarneys took a trip to Greenock, Scotland. All three were anxious to see where the McFarneys had come from. Egan didn't fully understand it, but it was important for him to see where his ancestor Eachann and Hilda, and their son Fergus had lived.

They found Eachann and Hilda's grave in the community cemetery and an odd feeling swept through Enos. A feeling he couldn't understand.

They walked the highlands as their ancestors had done before them. They took a train to Glasgow and visited the museum there and had lunch at a sidewalk café.

But after four days they were all in agreement, it was time to go home.

Egan and Enos would spend many days each week fishing for haddock. The market was even better now than Egan could remember as a boy.

Enos also spent more time looking for rocks along the shoreline. Only now he could identify most of them.

CHAPTER 18

Eno's four years in college had flown by him. His studies became more rugged with each passing year. He only dated some and saw no sense with sports. He was there to learn and he wanted to learn as much as he could in those four years.

His entire family was at his graduation. He didn't finish at the top of his class but he was two below the top. "So, what will you do now, Enos?" his sister Rachel asked.

"I have applied to the USGS for a position in the northeast; hopefully in Maine."

"Mom and Dad, I'll be home in the morning. The class is getting together afterwards."

* * *

Egan laid awake long into the night thinking about how to tell his son about the secret the family has held for over two hundred years. He fell into a restless sleep sometime around 2 a.m.

Before going to sleep, he had no idea what to do. But as soon as he woke in the morning the answer was clear. He was even happier than he had been in weeks.

Enos arrived home mid-morning. "Alison, would you fix a pot of coffee. The three of us need to talk and it is going to take a lot of coffee."

Egan was already seated in the living room and Enos came in and sat down. "What's up, Dad?"

"We'll wait for your mother."

She came in carrying a tray with three coffee cups and the pot.

Alison and Enos sipped their coffee and waited for Egan to start. He took another sip and said, "First, son, we are both so proud of you. The trust fund I promised you eight years ago I have already put into your account."

"Thank you, both of you."

"That was the easy part," he sipped more coffee and continued. He had both of their attention now.

"Alison, sweetheart—I have been keeping a secret from you and the family for many years. A secret that has been handed down from father to son for two hundred and twenty-four years. A secret that never has been violated or passed outside father and son. With one exception your seventh great grandmother, Enos, Innis. She and your seventh grandfather, Enig, created the secret and they had the secret as a codicil in their will that the secret was to be passed from father to son only. I am now breaking that promise because I think the time has come."

"What are you talking about, Egan?" Alison asked.

"The secret I am talking about is in that safe. Son, go over and open it. I will give you the combination. Start on zero and turn one full turn to the right and stop on zero." Enos did and waited. "Turn left and stop on fifty." He did, "Now turn right and stop on zero again and open the safe."

No one in the family was ever allowed to see what was kept in the safe. Alison's heart was racing as she waited to see what was there.

The door was open, "Take it out, son, and set it on the coffee table." He did

"Don't open it just yet. In 1770, our 7th great grandparents found this chest under the kidney rock. During the Revolutionary War and the War of 1812, they reburied the chest under the rock to keep it from falling into British hands." Enos and Alison were both awestruck. *What was so important that it had to be kept from the British?*

177

Egan looked first at Alison and then Enos. He had their attention. "Before I allow you to open the chest, I must have both of you promise that this must still be kept secret. Alison?"

"I promise."

"Me, too," Enos said.

"Okay, open it, son, and remove the scroll."

The scroll was laying on other papers and a lot of money. Enos picked the scroll up and held it gently in both hands. "Look at it, son."

Enos unrolled the scroll and asked, "What is this, Dad? It looks like gibberish. What does it say, Dad?"

"No one has ever been able to figure it out. No one knows if it might be directions to a buried treasure. Or it could be explaining the beginning of Creation or how life will eventually end." Enos handed it to his mother.

"This isn't paper. What is it?"

"I don't know that, either. Do you, son?"

"It isn't paper. My next guess would be vellum, but I don't think it is, though. What are the other papers in here, Dad?"

"A short history of our family and who the secret had been passed on to. Enig and Innis' original will. You will need to read it sometime."

"And this money? How much is in here?"

"Emergency funds. Fifty thousand dollars."

Enos let that ride and he picked up the chest looking at it. "This looks like it just came off a store shelf. I don't suppose you know how long it had been under the rock?"

"That's part of the mystery."

"This isn't wood or metal. I have no idea what this chest is made from.

"Enig and Innis were buried on both sides of the rock to ensure that the rock is never moved. I believe, somehow that rock plays a role in what is written on the scroll. Have either of you ever noticed the small dimple on the rock. It is located, as close as I can figure, in the exact center."

"That may be there for one of two reasons," Enos said. "A marker that something is buried under the rock or it could be a starting point to find something else."

"I'd like to see this dimple," Alison said.

"Before we leave, let's put the chest and scroll back in the safe," Egan said.

Egan showed them the dimple. "It is in the center," Alison said.

"The inside of this dimple is so smooth I don't think it was made by chisel," Enos said. "It's funny I have never noticed this before."

"Or me," Alison said.

They went back to the living room and drank more coffee while talking about the secret.

Alison said, "When you first said you had a family secret that had always been passed from father to son, I was feeling a little ostracized, left out. But I think I can understand now. Father to son, so it would always remain in the McFarney family, and the consequences if the secret was known by others.

"With your college education, son, I think you might be in a position to finally solve the mystery. Science is evolving faster now than ever before and I believe some day, in your lifetime, you will be able to use science's advancement to solve it. But until that time happens, I would suggest that you put this out of your mind or it will drive you crazy. I think you'll know when the time comes."

"Okay, but for now I would like to read through the will and the family history," Enos said.

"So would I," Alison said.

Enos opened the safe again and removed the chest. While they were reading the papers, Egan made lunch for all, soup and grilled cheese.

Later that day, Enos walked back out to the kidney rock,

thinking about the possibilities that might still be under the rock. But to look for them now might disrupt the natural order of discovering what the scroll had to say.

It took Enos two days to stop thinking about the chest and scroll. A week later he received his answer from the Maine Geological Office in Augusta.

"Yahoo! I've got the job. There is an opening in the mineral survey department. And if I want the job, I am to call the office immediately. Hell, yes, I want the job! Oh, excuse my language."

"That's okay, son. Make your call," Alison said.

"Oh wow, this is better than I even dreamed."

"What do you mean, son?" Egan asked.

"I'm to be at the Bangor office on the Hogan Road tomorrow morning at 8 a.m. And expect to start work. Boy, someone is surely looking out after me."

"I need to go to town to take care of things now," he said.

"Go ahead, son."

First he stopped at the bank to look at his trust fund and transfer some money to his checking. "Mr. Weber, I'd like to talk with you about my trust fund."

"Yes, certainly, Mr. McFarney. Step into my office." Mr. Weber gave Enos his balance sheet.

Enos looked at the balance and he couldn't believe his eyes. "Are these figures correct, Mr. Weber?"

"Yes they are, Mr. McFarney. You are a wealthy man."

"2.1 million dollars. I never imagined. Here's what I want to do with it, Mr. Weber. I want $50,000.00 in a simple savings account and the 2 million in a certificate of deposit and the remaining $50,000 in my checking account."

His next stop was at the men's clothing store for khaki pants and shirts, a pair of quality hiking shoes and a pair of fine leather boots. Then he drove home and said, "Mom and Dad, I want to take you out for supper tonight at Benson's Restaurant," —the finest restaurant in Belfast and probably the most expensive.

They dressed in evening attire and were given a table overlooking the bay. "We have never eaten here, Egan, this is so nice," Alison said.

A very petite, pretty waitress brought menus and said, "Good evening, folks, my name is Annriellia. Would you like something to drink before you order?"

Before his mother could say no, Enos said, "Yes, please, a bottle of Chateau St. Michelle."

"A very good choice, monsieur."

She was back in a few minutes and poured wine in each of their glass. "I'll give you a few minutes."

"We eat seafood all the time; I want a good beef steak," Alison said.

"That sounds good to me," Egan said.

"And me."

"That was a good choice. We have Argentine beef. The best beef in the world." They all had baked potato with sour cream and a green garden salad.

"I have never had wine before this," Alison said, "and it is very good. Maybe we should have some at home, sweetheart."

"We can do that."

Annriellia brought their steak dinners in on a cart. "The finest steak we have. Enjoy."

"Thank you," Egan said.

"Oh wow, this is the best tasting steak I have ever had," Egan said.

Alison and Enos agreed with him.

"We should dine here more often, sweetheart. It isn't like we can't afford it."

* * *

Enos was up early the next morning. He didn't want to e late for his first day at work. As he was leaving he said, "I'll be back this evening."

The USGS office was at the Bangor International Airport.

Not far from the terminal building.

The office manager, Bill Ingram, met Enos in the parking lot and the two talked for a few minutes before going inside. "You'll be working with John Jennings, project supervisor. I'll let him tell you what project he is working on now."

Inside he was introduced to John and pilot Alan Dufour. The three moved into a conference room.

There were charts and maps on the walls and a center conference table. "Sit down. Gentlemen, this is the new guy, Enos McFarney," John Jennings said, "This is pilot, Alan Dufour, and fellow geologist, Mike Hanson.

"Gentlemen, it has come to the attention of our mineral and mining department in the Department of Environmental Protection of increased mining activity, i.e. gold, in Canada and only a short distance from the Maine border. If you'll look at this chart, I have pinpointed the locations of these mines. You'll see, they are on the eastern, northern and western border of Maine and this one is in La Patrie, Quebec, only a few miles north of New Hampshire. These areas in Canada and Maine are under the Principal Paleozoic and Mesozoic folded areas, the same tectonic plate."

Mike Hanson spoke up, "Then there must be gold reserves all across northern Maine."

"That is exactly what the governor wants to know. Not to go out prospecting, but he and DEP want a clear digital map of most of the state of Maine. Beginning in northern Maine, on the western border.

"Enos, you are recently out of college; are you familiar with digital mapping and IR (infrared) spectrometers?"

"Yes, sir, I am."

"And the software for downloading the digital information to our computers for photomapping?"

"Yes, sir."

"Good."

"Gentlemen, we leave the Bangor Airport tomorrow at 7 a.m. Be here at 6:30 a.m. and we'll go over some last minute details. Bring one travel bag with enough clothes for a week. We'll be staying at the Clayton Village in T11-R14. That will be our base of operations and we'll stay in the hotel and take our meals in the hotel restaurant. Since the director of timberlands for IP has his own airplane, there'll be aviation gas available when we need it. I have already cleared everything with the IP's timberland's director, Bill Vestor. Any questions?"

There were none, "Good, I'll see you all here tomorrow morning."

Enos was hungry and there was a Burger King within walking distance of the office. He had a Whopper, fries and coffee.

When he finished, he walked back to the office and he was studying the wall maps and charts when the manager, Bill Ingram, walked into the room. "I thought you'd be on your way home, Enos."

"I wanted to look at these charts and maps some more and any other material I can find."

"John was busy this morning and he probably didn't show you to your office. Come, I'll show you. You'll share this office with Mr. Hanson. Supplies are in a smaller room at the end of the hall."

Ingram went back to his office and Enos went back to the conference room and found manuals on digital mapping. He wanted to refresh himself before the next day.

At home that evening, he told his folks all about what he would be doing for the next few weeks. And he had to explain how digital mapping worked. "We fly over the ground at low elevation and we drop a torpedo-like transmitter that is tethered to the plane. This transmitter sends radio waves into the ground as we fly and signals come back. Later when we are back in the office, we will plug this information into a computer with a special program, and it will produce a map of the area with the different mineral signatures. Each mineral has its own vibrational signature and this computer interprets this information and puts it in a map form."

"So someone in Augusta thinks there is gold in northern Maine?"

"Yes, and what I saw today, I would have to agree, even before we do the digital mapping."

"That's amazing," Alison said.

"Will they or you be able to tell how much gold is there?"

"No, the instruments will only indicate the presence of gold and other minerals."

"I'd like to see these maps after you make them," his dad said.

Before going to sleep that night, he packed his cordura overnight bag. Then he lay awake for a while, too excited about tomorrow to sleep.

* * *

Enos was the first to arrive at the USGS office, Supervisor Jennings, next. Once everyone was there, they loaded the gear in Jennings vehicle and drove out on the tarmac to load the plane. The plane, a de Havilland Beaver, could carry six passengers plus luggage. The Beaver had floats and wheels attached to the floats that could be lifted from within the cockpit when landing on water. The rear seats had been removed to allow room for the mapping equipment. Jennings sat up front with the pilot and Enos and Mike Hanson sat on the makeshift seats. "We'll be about an hour or so, so make yourselves comfortable back there." Jennings radioed the air traffic controller in the tower and was told to get in line behind the 737.

Twenty minutes later, they were air bound, heading north at an altitude of five thousand feet. "This is pretty smooth," Enos said.

"It is now," the pilot said, "The air is still cool. As soon as the air warms, we'll experience some turbulence."

Mr. Dufour must have flown this route before. At exactly one hour and ten minutes they landed on Clayton Lake and taxied up to the IP wharf. While Dufour was fueling the plane, the others removed their luggage from the plane. "You can put that in my pickup and I'll take them to the hotel for you; someone will take them to your rooms."

"Thanks, Bill," Jennings said.

"We should have enough time to make one pass north along the border and the return pass and by then, it'll be time for lunch," Dufour said.

They flew from the Reality Road north to Estcourt Station, following the boundary and staying inside the border by a quarter of a mile. When they came to Estcourt Station, Enos engaged the electric winch and brought the torpedo-like radio wave transmitter up. Dufour made a circle over Estcourt Station and flew the same pattern south setting over another quarter of a mile.

After lunch they continued flying the same pattern to Estcourt Station and back. They were only able to make one more pass and return.

Bill Vestor joined them for supper. "Well, what are you seeing?"

"Oh, we won't know that until we plug all this information into our home computer," Jennings said.

"I'll be interested to see what your computer has to say. I'll be flying out of here after breakfast tomorrow. I have a meeting in Bangor."

"By any chance could I fly back with you?" Jennings asked. "There is no need of all three of us in the airplane and it would free up some room."

"No problem, I'd welcome the company."

"Mike, you'll be in charge. We'll use the Reality Road as our south line. Then when the north section is done, we'll set down below the Reality Road to the Golden Road coming out of Greenville. Figure on being back in Bangor Friday afternoon at 6 p.m.

"I have heard Clayton Lake Village mentioned on the evening news, but I never realized it was an actual village in the middle of the wilderness," Enos said.

"We have a hotel/boarding house, restaurant, a small library, post office and a modern garage. The people who live here aren't seasonal occupants. This is their home," Bill said.

"How long has the village been here?" Enos asked.

"Since the 1920s in King LaCroix's days, Edward LaCroix. He brought the two ninety-ton locomotives to Eagle Lake, south of here. He now has a house on this side of the boarder near Lac Frontier. There's a lot of history up here in this wilderness, young fella," Bill said.

Dufour said, "When we set down south of here, we'll fly over the locomotives and I'll point them out to you."

Bill stood up away from the table and, "Gentlemen, tomorrow morning."

After supper, Enos walked down to the lakeshore. It was so quiet there. The only sounds were an occasional screen door slamming closed. He walked on the road towards the border. Soon he couldn't even hear the slamming doors. What a different world than what he had grown up in. One thing was for sure, when he could, he would buy some books about this area and learn some of the history.

* * *

The next morning, John Jennings left with Bill Vestor and the USGS crew took off to continue mapping the area. With one less crew member, there was more room in the plane.

That day they began making two passes in the morning and two complete round trip passes in the afternoon. On Thursday, the air was slightly rough and each pass was taking longer. After making the first pass in the afternoon, dark storm clouds were moving in from the northwest.

"We'll have to suspend anymore passes today. Once we reach the Reality Road, I'm heading for Clayton Lake," Pilot Dufour said.

Before reaching the Reality Road they were encompassed with driving rain and dark clouds. "Bring the transmitter onboard. We can't go any further in this weather. I'm putting down at the Red Pine landing strip. It is dead ahead. Fasten your seatbelts. I'm not able to swing around and land into the wind. We have to go in with it. No choice."

"Wow, listen to that rain hitting the fuselage. We made it down just in time," Dufour said.

"Now what do we do?" Enos asked.

"We wait. Mike and I had to spend ten hours inside the plane once two years ago."

Enos looked at Mike and he nodded his head.

"As quick as this came in, I bet it'll blow out just as quick," Dufour said. "I hope."

When the rain stopped and the dark clouds blew out, they returned to Clayton Lake.

The next day, Friday, they made two flights in the morning and one in the afternoon. Now it was time to go home for the weekend.

Enos and his folks stayed up late that night. They both wanted to hear all about his first week on the job and about the early history of Clayton Lake Village.

The next day, he drove to Bangor to Border's Bookstore, and bought every book he could find about the history of the northern Maine wilderness.

He tired to explain to his folks how big the northern wilderness was, but he knew one would have to see it for themselves in order to understand. "And there is so much history there. I don't know why it is not taught in school."

* * *

Enos took two books with him back to Clayton Village and he'd stay up late reading them.

While the crew was mapping more of the northern wilderness, John Jennings had taken the digital information from the previous week and loaded it into the computer. It didn't take long for the computer to print out a map of minerals found. Not a map per se, but by the elemental digital signature. The results were not shocking, but they certainly were interesting. What he found along the St. John watershed was most interesting.

The crew were six weeks flying and mapping the territory north of the Reality Road all the way to the New Brunswick border, and there Jennings found another interesting spot on the map. Along the border and Presque Isle there was the familiar gold signature and not that far away from a New Brunswick gold mine across the border from Easton.

The first of August they started mapping south of the Reality to the Golden Road out of Millinocket. They stayed at the Shin Pond Village cabins and took their meals in the small restaurant in the general store/office building. They left the plane at night at Scotty's flying service just down over the hill. He also had aviation gas.

When Jennings downloaded this information he was again surprised to find such a gold signature from the New Brunswick border twenty miles inland to the west. And again along the Quebec border, between St. Zacharie and Jackman.

Enos was beginning to wish that this digital mapping would soon come to an end. He would rather have been doing some groundwork.

* * *

They flew over Washington County, mapping south of Baxter Park to Dover, and the western mountains to New Hampshire and Rumford. There were a few key areas Jennings had them fly over again. This time east and west. The Oakfield Hills, Brandy Pond area in T7-R4, Washington County and the

188

western mountains north of Umbagog Lake. And in particular, a section of T7-R5 from the top of the hill in Moro Plt. to Umcolus Lake. Here, to strengthen the digital information. They spent four hours flying this section.

It was the end of October when they finished. They spent the rest of that year and the winter of 1995 working with the computers printing out maps of that entire area with first the elements digital signature and then color coded maps showing mineral deposits.

Finally by early April, they had all of the digital information mapped and printed as handouts to each member plus a large wall chart with the same information.

Mr. Jennings called for a meeting in the conference room, with the manager, Bill Ingram. "That is impressive, John. I guess after seeing this, everyone's suspicion about the possibility of gold is now quite apparent. Excuse me, John, this is your meeting."

"It is easy to see where the heaviest deposits are located. Even though this chart shows significant placements of gold, it does not in any way suggest how much there is or the quality. That would require drilling samples.

"But this also shows where there could be possible oil deposits. Again, there is no way of telling how large the deposit would be, only that there is an oil signature. That's why I'm sending Mike and Enos up Monday to collect rock samples and take core samples around East Hasting Brook in Merrill Township and in the Brandy Pond area in T7-R4 and in the area of Allagash River and the confluence of Big Brook in T15-R10.

"I'll send them up Monday morning. Plan on staying over at Dean's Hotel in Portage. You may end up staying two nights, depending on how much trouble you have finding Allagash and Big Brook."

"I was going to send all this information to DEP and the governor, but now I think I'll wait until you have the statistics."

* * *

At home Friday evening, Enos showed his folks the color coded charts of his work. "This is unbelievable that that much gold could exist and no one is mining it."

"Well, DEP's regulations are so strict, mining companies can't operate."

"But this chart is impressive."

The next day Enos drove back to Bangor and bought a new GMC extended cab four-wheel drive pickup; silver over indigo blue color.

Enos spent a lot of time that weekend talking with his folks. "How is the boat business?"

"They stopped making fishing boats and dingies and only make the more expensive luxury yachts. The company is making money. At least Edward and Paul are spending money like they are making a lot. They each have bought pricey mansions on the coast and they and wives are always taking vacations.

"What will you be working on now, son?" Alison asked.

"Mike and I are driving back up north Monday and do some groundwork where we found strong signatures for oil. We'll be staying in Portage at Dean's Hotel. Jennings said plan on two nights at Dean's."

"You sure do have an interesting job."

During the weekend, Enos noticed how much his folks had slowed down. They both used to be so active. They each would turn sixty-five soon and maybe it was, time to slow down some.

They took Enos' new pickup on the trip north. They stopped at Whitey's Market for gas and they were able to buy sandwiches there for lunch.

"What are you boys up to today?" Linda asked.

"There's a rock formation we want to look at near Brandy Pond," Enos said. They had been told not to spread the information.

"Do you know how to find Brandy Pond?" she asked.

"Follow this road to Smyrna Mills, about three quarters of a mile. Drive across the four-way intersection to Rt212. Follow that five miles and there will be a wide gravel road on the right. There is a gate but it stays open. Follow the gravel road across Dudley Deadwater and take the 2nd road on the right. That'll take you as close to Brandy as you can drive."

"Thank you."

They continued on, "Who needs a road map when you have people like that to help you," Mike said.

They found the road and stopped on the deadwater bridge. "There's a large moose," Enos said. Just then, two young calves stood up.

They drove on and found the road to Brandy. Before coming to the end of the road, they drove through a marsh area then up on higher ground. The road ended in a short distance.

They got out and started looking for rocks. They hiked out on a few skidder trails and didn't find anything interesting.

Back on the other side of the marsh, where the road split around Big Brawn Mt., there was some disturbed gravel that had not been laid down for the road.

"This is more like what we have been looking for," Mike said.

There were many old brownish-orange colored rocks that could be crumbled in your hand. "These rocks tell us there is oil underneath," Mike said.

"These rocks must be four to five hundred million years old," Enos said.

They filled a bucket and left. Taking the other road around Big Brawn which brought them back to the Dudley Deadwater Road.

Mike was navigating and said, "We turn right when we're back on Rt. 212. After we cross Hastings Brook there is a dirt road on the right that goes out to East Hastings Deadwater. It looks like a dead end road."

"Yeah, in a gravel pit."

"An old one. This will be good."

They parked the pickup and started looking at the rocks that had accumulated at the bottom. "Look, Enos, the same brownish-orange crumbly rock we found near Brandy."

"These rocks are all over the place."

They half filled a bucket and started looking for other rocks. "You know, Mike, we forgot to take core samples from Brandy."

"We'll have to go back after we're through here."

They took two core samples at the bottom of the pit bank at each end of the pit and two more out in the marsh. They labeled the core samples and put them in the truck.

They drove back to the Brandy Road and took two samples. One where they had found the old rocks, and one out in the shaded wet land. "There, we can go now."

They stopped on the bridge at Dudley Deadwater to eat lunch. "I don't see the moose out there now."

"Holy shit!" Enos looked in his rearview mirror and saw a huge loaded log truck barreling down on them. With his air horn blaring, "Big damn truck!"

He put it in gear and floored it. Just in time. Mike turned around to look. "Look at all the dust he is stirring up. I wouldn't stop if I were you."

They beat footed it out to Rt. 212 with the log truck practically pushing them. "That was close," Mike said,

"Yeah, too close. Lesson learned."

They drove back to East Hastings Deadwater for lunch. They sat on the tailgate eating. "I wonder why no one has ever drilled this for oil. I can't believe there isn't at least one petroleum company that knows about this," Mike said.

"Maybe they do and they can't work with DEP. Look at the mineral signatures that we found and not one of those locations has ever been mined. The state is rich with minerals. My guess would be the companies can't work with DEP's restrictions. Maybe someday, but not now."

* * *

From East Hastings Deadwater they drove to Dean's Hotel in Portage. By the time they unpacked and washed up, it was time for supper.

Before going to bed, they studied the Maine Gazetteer book. "Looks like we'll have to take a few different roads to get there because of bridges that are out. And then we'll probably have to do some hiking."

The next morning, they left the hotel early and started out the Fish Lake Road. They came to the Fish River check point and were stopped at a closed gate. A pretty young woman came out of the building and asked, "What is your destination please?"

"Big Brook in T15-R10."

"Will you be wanting a campsite?"

"No, we'll be back out this afternoon."

"Are you going to do any fishing? I don't see any fishing gear."

"No fishing; we are geologists for the USGS and we're here to collect rock samples near Big Brook and the Allagash River."

"I guess there'll be no charge. Remember the log trucks own the road and they have the right of way." She lifted the gate and let them pass. They met log truck after log truck. "What time do these guys start work anyhow?" Enos asked.

"It must be before we were out of bed."

For a while they followed the well-traveled road. There were no road signs in this country. Enos pulled to a stop when they came to a Y in the road. The St. Francis Road was on the right. "I think we want to go left, Enos."

"You know someone could very easily get lost out here."

"Wow, look at this load coming, Mike." Enos pulled as far to the side as he could. The truck went by in a cloud of dust and he had to wait for the dust to settle before continuing.

"He had enough on that load for two trucks," Mike said.

After several turns onto adjacent roads, they finally made their way to the washed out bridge on Big Brook. He left the pickup off the road, and with a bucket and rock hammers they started following the brook to the Allagash River. It was more than a mile hike.

In the river, they found mostly dark colored igneous rock. They waded around in the shallows and didn't see anything but igneous rock. They checked Big Brook itself and found the same. "What we need is to go back to that gravel pit we passed on the Big Brook Road," Mike said.

"Let's take a core sample about a hundred feet from the brook and river. What we need is to find some metamorphic rock and not igneous," Enos said

They drove to the gravel pit they had passed coming in earlier, but the pit was too new. "What we need is an old pit, like the one we found at East Hastings Deadwater."

They turned around in the other direction checking all old and new side roads. Then two miles away they found what they wanted. An old pit growing up with alder bushes.

They were able to fill a bucket with brownish-orange crumbly rock. They could crush the rocks in their hands. And they took two core samples. "I think we're done here, let's see if we can find our way back," Mike said.

"I hope we don't get behind one of those log trucks," Enos said.

* * *

They had breakfast Wednesday morning and then they drove back to the office in Bangor. Then they cataloged and labeled the samples. The next few days they would analyze the rock samples, and the core samples would be shipped to a better equipped laboratory in the New England USGS office in Boston.

The first thing Enos did when he was home was to wash

his pickup. His dad said, "Your new pickup was so dirty, I didn't know who was driving in."

While they ate supper, Enos told his folks all about his trip up north and the extra big log trucks. "Those truck drivers claim their share of the road right down the center of the road."

CHAPTER 19

Four more years had passed and Enos was now well grounded in USGS. He and his partner, Mike Hanson, had trekked over much of the state, mapping and checking and rechecking their findings before downloading the information in the computer.

He had worn out the GMC pickup and he bought a new one. His mom and dad had slowed and were feeling their age at seventy and Enos found a single, retired nurse, Betty Hargrove, that agreed to move in to take care of Egan and Alison. To his surprise, neither objected.

Ms. Hargrove was very much at home with the McFarneys, and besides taking care of them and the house, she made it clear to both of them that they were to walk to town and back every day. She walked with them just in case.

But Egan had for two years now been experiencing some angina. Only slight pains at first but over time they became more severe. Sometimes he would go for days without any pain.

He hid the pain attacks well, for two years Alison never suspected anything, but Ms. Hargrove wasn't so easy to fool. When she'd ask if he was alright, he'd say, "Just a nerve in my spine being pinched."

Enos was home the first weekend in May and that morning before anyone was up Egan had a severe heart attack. Alison hollered for Ms. Hargrove and Enos. Betty immediately called 911 for an ambulance.

Egan was conscious and motioned with his hand for Enos to come close. "Yes, Dad, I'm right here," and he held his hand and Alison held his other hand.

"Son—find answers. Don't—wait no longer." Enos knew what his dad was saying and he said, "I will, Dad," and he lightly squeezed his hand.

Egan turned to look at his wife, Alison, and said, "—always loved you so much," and he squeezed her hand, closed his eyes and rested forever.

Enos took two weeks off to take care of the family affairs. Practically the entire town had closed the businesses to attend Egan's funeral. There were so many people the ceremony had to be held outside. Like his ancestors, Egan's body was cremated and his ashes buried in the family plot behind the house and in front of the kidney rock.

Alison had a very difficult time accepting Egan's passing. "He was so much a part of me. I don't know if I can go on without him."

Ms. Hargrove was very beneficial to Alison's well-being. The two acted like sisters. During the day Alison was okay, as long as Betty was there with her. But alone at night—the nights were long and lonesome.

One day in the middle of June, Betty said, "Enos, I hate to say this but your mother has no will to live. She is slipping a little each day. She misses your father so much."

"Thank you for telling me, Betty. All we can do, then, is see that she is comfortable."

By July 1st, Alison had more or less willed herself into a peaceful forever sleep. And like her husband, practically the entire town showed up at the funeral and her ashes were placed next to Egan's in the family plot.

Enos gave Betty Hargrove a sizeable bonus for taking care of his mother. He went back to work, but he couldn't keep his mind on his work. One night while sitting on the porch watching lightning bugs, he remembered what his father had said just before he died.

He spent most of the night on the porch thinking about the chest and scroll.

"Perhaps the time has come to solve this."

Some time around 3 a.m. he managed to fall asleep for two hours. When he woke he could remember a dream. A woman, a school and books. The dream had been very pleasing, but this was all he could recall of it now. He dressed and drove to the office in Bangor without eating breakfast.

"Mr. Ingram, do you have a moment?"

"Certainly, Enos. Come in. Now what can I do for you?"

"This is difficult for me to ask, but I need an extended leave of absence. At least a year, sir."

"Are you looking to relocate, Enos?"

"No, nothing like that. I enjoy working here and after the absence I hope I can come back."

"Can you give me an idea why you are requesting a leave of absence?"

"There isn't much that I can say, only that I need to take care of some family business."

"Certainly, you can have your leave. You're a good man, Enos, and I surely hope you will come back."

"I intend to, sir."

Mr. Ingram stood up then to shake hands with Enos. "Will you explain my absence to Jennings and Hanson?"

From there, Enos drove up to the University of Maine at Orono, to the administration's office. "Mr. Philbrook, may I talk with you for a few minutes?" Enos asked.

"Mr. Philbrook, my name is Enos McFarney and I am an alumni and I am hoping you can point me in the right direction. I need to talk with the best linguist in the country."

"That's easy. Dr. Inez Ferguson at the Halifax Language Institute of Canada. She is the best in the western hemisphere.

Would you like her telephone number? This is her cell number."

"Yes. Thank you."

"Can I ask what this is all about, Mr. McFarney?"

"It's a document that has been in my family for more than two hundred years and no one has been able to read it."

"Well, I'm sure Inez Ferguson will be able to help you."

"Thank you, Mr. Philbrook."

Enos still hadn't eaten anything yet and he drove home and called Ferguson's cell number. She answered on the first ring. "Hello."

"Mrs. Ferguson? Inez Ferguson?"

"Yes and it is Ms. Ferguson."

"Ms. Ferguson, this is Enos McFarney from Belfast, Maine, and it is very important that I meet with you as soon as possible."

"What can I do for you, Mr. McFarney?"

"I have an old document that I need deciphered."

"I can look at it, but I make no guarantee. When can you drive up to Halifax?"

"I'll be on the 6 a.m. Nova Scotia Ferry in the morning."

"Okay. I'll meet you in the terminal parking lot. I'll be driving a red Toyota Rav 4."

"I'll have a silver blue GMC pickup."

"Tomorrow morning, Mr. McFarney."

"Thank you and goodbye."

He was excited, maybe someone will be able to decipher the scroll. He was hungry, but too excited to fix supper. He drove out to the Burger King.

* * *

The next morning at 5:30 a.m., Enos drove his pickup onto the ferry and locked it and went up on the observation deck at the Bar Harbor ferry terminal. It was an eight-hour trip but it wouldn't be as tiring. He would be there at 2 p.m.

The ferry was fully loaded. All going to Halifax. It was a

perfect day for an ocean trip. The sky was blue and the ocean was calm. Even though the crossing was nice, he was extremely anxious.

Halifax Harbor was now in sight and the CAT ferry began to slow the approach.

Before he drove off the ferry he spotted the red Rav 4. There was a pretty, country-style woman standing beside it. Smiling.

He pulled in next to her and got out. "Ms. Ferguson, I presume?"

"Yes and you must be Mr. McFarney."

"Enos, please."

"Okay, and I am Inez." They shook hands and they held hands for a brief moment longer than usual. They each could feel something from the other as they clasped hands. They looked directly at each other. "Excuse me for staring. Just for a second I thought you looked a little familiar. Have you ever been in Halifax before?"

"No, this is the first time."

"Why don't you follow me to the institute."

It wasn't a long drive, but there was a lot of traffic.

She thought it was unusual for him to be bringing his travel bag in with him. She took him down to her office and closed the door. "Now, Enos, what can I do for you?"

He removed the chest from his travel bag and set it on top of the desk for now. "Inside of this chest is a scroll, a document that has been in my family for a long time. And no one has been able to decipher it."

He removed a folder from his travel bag. "What I am about to say next may seem strange to you at first."

"Go ahead."

"Before I show you the document, I would first like you to read and sign this non-disclosure agreement," And he handed it to her.

She read it and asked, "Why do you think this non-disclosure agreement is necessary."

"That will become obvious—I hope, once you see it. I have no idea what it could be. A treasure map, some secret agreement between two ancient powers. I have no idea and it must be kept a secret. My family has kept the secret for a long, long time."

"Okay, I'll agree. You certainly have piqued my curiosity." She signed and dated it.

Enos opened the chest. Inez was holding her breath. He removed some papers first and then the scroll and handed it to her.

She unrolled it and gasped, "Oh my. I have never seen anything like this before. And the scroll isn't paper. It might be vellum, but I'm not even sure about that. I recognize some of the writing. It is the old-style Scottish brogue. But not all of it. And I don't know what else is with it."

"Tell me about your family. Where did they come from?"

"In 1770, my seventh great grandparents moved from Greenock, Scotland, to Belfast, Maine."

"Do you know if either of them could write and speak the old brogue?"

"It is in the back that the keepers of the secret would write. My 7th great grandad, Enig, could talk using the old dialect, but he couldn't write or read it. During the Revolutionary War with England, he was confronted once by an English man of war ship. He was in a fishing boat carrying dispatches to Boston and he spoke in the brogue dialect so the English couldn't understand him. They let him pass.

"No one in the family has ever been able to read even a little."

"Make yourself comfortable and I'll load this into my computer."

As she was typing she said, "For now I'll have to eliminate the strange symbols and words and see what the computer comes up with."

"I don't suppose there would be a coffee machine anywhere?"

"Yes, turn right out this door and then left at the first intersection. You'll see the vending machines. I would like a cup also, please, cream no sugar."

He was back in five minutes. "This is good coffee," he said.

"I'm almost finished."

"There, done. If you'll come here I'll explain what I have done. I typed it just as it is, leaving blank spaces for the unknown symbols. I am in the Scottish dialect program; lets see what it says."

She pressed enter and the two waited. "This may take a few minutes."

They sipped their coffee and she asked, "What do you do for work, Enos?"

"I'm a geologist for the United States Geological Survey Administration."

"Did you follow the family to geology?"

"No, I'm the first. My seventh great grandfather started building fishing boats in Greenock, Scotland, and when his son Enig moved his family to Belfast he started building fishing boats again."

"Does your family still build fishing boats?"

"No, my two older brothers own the company now and they build luxury yachts."

The printer started printing pages. "I guess we're done as far as we can go now," Inez said.

Enos stood behind her reading over her shoulder. "This is obviously a key to finding something else, but without the symbols translated there is no telling what it says. Those symbols were put in the document to keep people from understanding what is being said. Whoever wrote this didn't want the wrong people to decipher it."

"Can you translate the symbols?"

"Yes, but not today. The institute closes at 4 p.m."

Enos looked at his watch and said, "We have another hour; it is only 3 o'clock."

"You didn't set your watch ahead. The time zone changes at the border. Come, we have to leave. I'll save this in my computer. No one else can open it without my password.

As he was putting the scroll back in the chest and the chest in his travel bag, Inez said, "You can leave everything here. I'll lock my door."

"I'll feel more comfortable taking it with us. There's more to the story that I haven't told you yet."

"Okay."

Out in the parking lot Inez asked, "Did you make a reservation at a hotel before coming here?"

"No."

"Then I doubt if you'll be able to find a room within fifty miles of here this weekend. This is a special lobster, clam and seafood festival each summer. Hundreds of people from afar come for the entire weekend.

"You might think me a little forward, but I have a comfortable couch. You can stay with me."

"I would like that. Are you hungry? I'm starved."

"Follow me back to my home and then we can leave both vehicles there and walk to the festival."

She didn't live far away He carried his travel bag inside with him. "This originally was a two bedroom home. One bedroom is office and computer."

He set his bag on the couch. "This is a nice house, and close to the institute."

They both washed up and then after locking the house, they walked down to the festival. There were a dozen outfits cooking lobster and clams. "How do you like your lobster?" Inez asked.

"Growing up at home once in a while the family would

have a lobster and clam cookout. Steamed in seaweed."

"Then I know just the spot and we can have some free wine also."

"Why is the wine free?"

"Mr. Charles makes it himself. Not to sell, but only for the festival. He can't legally sell it, but he can give it away. Wait until you taste it. Then tell me what it is made from."

Mr. Charles was set up right on the sandy shore. "Hello, Inez, been looking for you," Mr. Charles said.

"Hello, Charles."

Charles looked at Enos and said, "Hmm, you never before showed up here with a boyfriend, Inez. Something new?"

For Charles benefit, she leaned over and kissed Enos. "Oh wow—that was pretty good," she said. "Can you do it again?" All the time Charles was watching.

"I don't know what came over me. That first kiss was for Charles' benefit. He has never seen me here with a man before."

"You kiss really nice, Inez."

"Charles—can we have some of your wine?"

"You sure can, Inez," Charles said, while chuckling. He poured each a glass full.

Enos smelled the wine first. "It has a nice fragrance."

"Taste it," Inez said. She was already sipping hers.

Enos did, several sips. "It has an extraordinary flavor. Very nice. I don't think it is made with grapes." He took another sip. "I don't have any idea."

"Okay if I tell him, Charles?" He nodded his head it was okay. "Chokecherry and rhubarb."

"I never would have guessed. It is very good."

"How much longer, Charles?" she asked.

"Ten minutes. Have another glass of wine while you wait."

"If I'm not mistaken, Inez, you are Scottish, correct?"

"Yes, my great grandparents came over in 1820 from Glasglow."

"Inez Ferguson."

"Yes?"

"My 6th great grandmother was Innis, she married Enig and their son was Fergus. Innis was spelled different I-n-n-i-s."

"I don't believe in coincidences," Inez said, "never have."

There platters of lobster and clams and hot butter and biscuits was brought to them.

"Thank you, Charles." More people were beginning to come.

"Oh, wow," he said. "I haven't tasted anything this good since our family cookout."

"I could eat this every day," Inez said, "but I probably would look like a pickle barrel."

They ate in silence enjoying their food and wine.

People were beginning to wait in line now for a table. "We got here just in time, I'd say," Enos said. "Maybe we should leave so someone else can sit. Where do we pay for the meal and wine?"

"There is no set amount. There is a kettle where we leave and people just make a donation."

"What a unique way to do business." Enos left fifty dollars; the meal and wine were surely worth it. "Thank you, Mr. Charles."

"You take good care of Inez, you hear."

"I will."

They walked along the shore when they could. There was easy listening music playing somewhere. "Enos, are you married or anything?"

"No wife, no kids."

"A girlfriend?"

"No."

"You?" he asked.

"Never been married, no kids, no boyfriend."

"Glad we got that out of the way," he said in a good way.

"I'm thirty years old," he said.

"Me too."

They had to leave the shore and started walking through the many vendor displays. "Your family?" Enos asked.

"Only child since I was fifteen. My folks left me enough money to support myself while I worked on my doctorate degree."

They found the music. A band was playing in the center of four streets that had been blocked off to traffic. They found seats where they could rest and listen to the music. "There's a bar over there," Inez said, "And I would like some more wine."

"I'll be right back."

He returned a few minutes later with two glasses of wine. "Is this festival only one day or does it continue?"

"Friday, Saturday and Sunday they all begin to pick up."

"This is good wine, but I liked Charles' wine better. I never tasted anything like it."

He put his glass down, stood up and took her hands and she stood up. "Dance?"

There was no other couples dancing, but Enos thought this was a good time. Soon other couples were also dancing. "You dance well," she whispered in his ear.

"It feels good to hold you close," and he held her a little tighter, only enough so she could feel it. She did.

After the dance and the wine they started walking around again. They found two more seats overlooking the harbor.

"When do you have to be back to work?" she asked.

"I took a year leave of absence."

She smiled. "You think it'll take that long to solve this?"

"I don't know. Just in case."

"There's a cool breeze blowing in now. I think we should start back."

Enos walked with his arm around her. She didn't pull away.

"You're going to think this is corny, but I feel like we have known each other for a long time."

"I know what you mean. When I first touched your hand when we first met, I felt something like electricity passing from you to me."

By the time they were back at Inez's house, the ocean breeze had now started to blow stronger and the temperature had dropped. "This is a nice house, how long have you owned it?"

"I've been here five years and I rent.

"Sit down and make yourself comfortable, Enos, I'll get us some wine."

She brought two glasses of wine in and sat beside him on the couch. "You said something earlier, when we were in my office that there's more to this mystery. Is there?"

"Yes, there is a little, but I think I'll wait until you have deciphered the rest of the scroll."

"Okay, I'll ask no more questions until then."

"You told me earlier your father was a fisherman; is that how he died?"

"No, my folks were together. It was in the winter and the car slid off an icy hill and overturned in a ravine."

"You were only fifteen, you said. What did you do? I mean you couldn't have been by yourself."

"No, my mother had a sister here in Halifax and I lived with her until I went to college. Then she moved back to Glasglow. She never liked living in Nova Scotia."

Then on another note she said, "My dad had a McFarney boat. He said it was the best boat he ever owned."

"What brought your family to Nova Scotia?"

"My grandfather wanted to see the new world," she sipped her wine. "I wonder if our ancestors knew each other in the old country?"

"Perhaps, but there's no way of knowing."

They talked for a long time, getting to know each other and finishing that bottle of wine. Inez was tired and she leaned over and rested her head on his shoulders. "Boy—do I feel mellow," she said almost in a whisper.

"Come on Inez, I think it is time for you to go to bed." He took her hands and she stood up, looking at him and smiling. Then he kissed her ever so softly at first. Then she responded

"Oh boy—that kiss was better than the first kiss." She kissed him now. Then she pulled back and smiled and said, "I—would like to ask you to my bed. But—not yet."

She melted in his embrace. "Come on, Inez, I'll help you to your bedroom." She didn't move. She kept holding onto him. He bent down and picked her up in his arms and carried her into her bedroom and set her on her bed.

She was already asleep. He stood there for a moment then he decided he couldn't just leave her like this. He removed her blouse and skirt and after some finagling he was able to get her under the covers and pull them up under her chin. She was smiling.

* * *

Enos woke to the smell of coffee and bacon the next morning. "Do I have time for a shower, Inez?"

"Make it a quick one."

He did and he shaved. Breakfast was ready.

As they were eating, Enos said, "I had a wonderful time last night."

"So did I. I can't remember when I enjoyed myself so much."

After they had finished breakfast, Inez said, "I need to shower before we go to the institute."

"I'll take care of the dishes."

When she came out of her bedroom wearing clean clothes, Enos had the dishes done, dried and put away. Inez didn't say anything, but she surely noticed.

"This is Saturday and we'll probably be the only people in the institute today."

In her office, Enos took the chest out of his travel bag and put it on a desk and removed the scroll document. "Where do we start?" he asked.

"I'll download these symbols into the computer and see if I can get a language identity."

It took her a few minutes and then she only did a few of the symbols. Enough so the computer would recognize them.

While she was typing Enos was watching over her shoulder and she asked, "Did you put me in bed last night?"

"Yes, you said it was time to go to bed and when you stood up we kissed."

"I remember kissing you. But not much after that."

"You were about to fall asleep in my arms, so I carried you into your bedroom. You were sound asleep when I laid you down."

"Did you undress me?"

"Yes. I didn't feel right just leaving you in your clothes lying on top of the bed. I removed your blouse and skirt and got you under the covers."

"Ummm, I knew I was being undressed, but when I woke in the morning I thought it only a dream. Until I realized I still had my underclothes on." And then she added, "Thank you."

"Here comes our answer. Just what I thought it might be. Norwegian. But it is the old style Nor language. Like most of the document is old Scottish brogue."

"Can you translate it?"

"Yes, and it'll take time. What we'll have to do is take each individual phrase and enter that for a translation and each one, one at a time. This might take all day."

"Is there anything I can do to help?"

"A cup of coffee would be good."

He was back in a few minutes with two coffees. As he drank his coffee he kept moving around the office. The anticipation was too much for him. "Enos, why don't you go for a walk around the grounds. This is going to take me quite a while. And your pacing isn't helping any. Here, here's my key to let yourself back in."

Before going outside, he roamed around inside the institute. He found the science lab particularly interesting. Looking through the window in the door he could see some instruments. One particular stood out, a mass spectrometer. With that instrument he would be able to determine what material the document and the chest were.

He also recognized a laser ablation device. Used to remove small microscopic particles to be scanned. There were more instruments and devices but from the window he wasn't able to identify them.

From there he found an exit in the rear and went outside to walk around the grounds.

While the computer was working, Inez was thinking about the night before. It felt so good when Enos undressed her. And she surely thought it had been a dream and not for real. A dream she didn't want to stop. And why didn't he take my underwear off too? That would really have been some dream. And she started laughing out loud.

Just then Enos was back. "I have some of it deciphered. But I haven't put in the document yet. It may take all afternoon to do the entire document. We may have to come back tomorrow.

"I know one thing, Enos, whoever wrote this was a wizard.

"While the computer is working, we might as well get something to eat. I'll lock the office door and I have the only key."

He followed her to the institute's staff cafeteria. There was a vending machine where they had a choice of soup or canned spaghetti. They each chose a can of chicken noodle soup and warmed it in a microwave.

"How many people know about the document and chest?"

"Right now—only you and I. For years, through the different generations, this was passed down from father to son only. That is until my father passed it to me. Then he asked my mother to join us. He said it was time to tell her about the family secret."

"I know there is more you aren't telling me, but I'll wait until you are ready."

* * *

By 4 o'clock that afternoon the computer had finished translating the Norwegian symbols. "There, we have this much. Now I'll have to insert the translation into the rest of the document. And I'm afraid that'll have to wait until Monday. No one, not even staff, is allowed in on Sunday during summer break."

As they walked back to Inez's house, she said, "I feel like I've walked a hundred miles today."

"Would you rather eat in instead of Mr. Charles?"

"Oh, I'm not that tired. But I would like to lay down for an hour."

She went straight to her bedroom, kicking her shoes off in the living room, took Enos by the hand, and said, "You need to lay down for an hour, too."

He lay on his back and she snuggled in close. They lay there probably thinking about the same. Inez knew he had a lot on his mind concerning what the document would finally reveal. But she was thinking she had never been so happy. And at the same time, they had only known each other for a day and a half. Nevertheless, she was still very happy. And there was another question. *What happens when he has his answer? Does he simply leave and that's all there is?*

Neither one said anything for an hour. They were enjoying the touch and the feel of a warm body lying next to them.

"Are you hungry?" he asked.

"Yes."

"I think we should get up. But first." He half rolled over to face her. She was smiling and he kissed her. With their lips still touching she said, "I'm hungry."

"Are there any stores open tomorrow?"

"There is a Kmart on the outskirts of Halifax. What do you need?"

"I only brought one change of clothes."

They were the first patrons of Mr. Charles again. "Hello, Charles," Inez said.

"Glad to see you back. Both of you. It'll be another ten minutes. Help yourself to the wine."

While Inez was filling two glasses. Charles stepped over beside her and said, "Inez, you look so happy. More so than yesterday. Don't lose him. He's good for you."

"I'll work on it, Charles."

As they waited for their lobster and clams, they enjoyed their wine. "This is a nicer evening than yesterday. No ocean breeze."

"It is nice. You know I remember some years there'd be rain and wind," she said.

"I would imagine the winters would be cold and raw being right on the coast."

"They usually are. Someday I'd like to take a trip to a South Seas Island Resort."

"I bet the food wouldn't be any better than Charles steamed lobster and clams. And I doubt if they would have such a fantastic wine. I might try making some, some day."

Charles brought their meal over and refilled their glasses. Still they were the only ones.

Before they had finished eating every table was full. "I guess that's our cue to leave," she said and finished her wine.

He left another fifty dollars for Charles. Inez saw how much he had left and said, "You don't have to leave that much."

"It was worth every penny. Besides I was with the prettiest girl around."

They walked down where a different band was playing this

evening and found the same seats and ordered more wine. The music was soft melodies and not rock and the amplifiers were not turned up so loud that the music was blasted at the audience.

"I have been working all day on an idea, Inez."

"Is that why you have been so quiet?"

"Partly. What do you do during the summer when you aren't working at the institute?"

"Nothing special."

"Do you have any plans for next week or the next?"

"No."

"Well, here's my idea. I would like you to come home with me. There is a lot you want to know about the chest and document. I can show you part of the secret at the same time as I'm telling you. That's one reason. The other reason is I wouldn't want to leave and just say thanks and goodbye. I really like you, Inez."

"How long?"

"Let's decide that one day at a time."

Again this evening they began to dance and soon other couples were also. As they were dancing she said, "I would be happy to go back with you for however long we decide."

"I'm so glad."

* * *

They left the festival and the music band earlier this evening and walked home. Before going in Enos hugged her and she offered her lips for a kiss. "Let's go in."

There was enough illumination from the streetlights so they didn't have to turn on any inside lights. They stood in the living room in front of the picture window for several moments gazing into the others eyes. She said, "I have never felt this way before," she smiled and he kissed her very softly at first. It was soon clear she wanted more passion.

He carried her into the bedroom and laid her on the bed. "That dream I thought I was having last night—make it come true now."

* * *

They both woke up Sunday morning with a smile. "That was great last night. Better than a kiss," she said.

They lay there for a few minutes simply enjoying the touch of closeness of each other. When they did get up she pulled on a robe and said, "You can have the shower first and I'll cook breakfast."

Breakfast was hot oatmeal and toasted English muffins.

After Inez showered and dressed, she said, "Let's go shopping."

His pickup was behind her car so she said, "It might be easier if I drive, since I know my way around the city. If you trust me with your pickup."

"Absolutely."

Kmart was located in a large shopping center on the western edge of the city. He picked out a pair of khaki pants, socks and underwear and Inez picked out two casual shirts that would match.

A lifelong friend of Inez was at the checkout. "Good morning, Sue."

"Hello, Inez, my you sure are glowing this morning." Then she looked at Enos and the two women smiled as they each shared a mental thought.

"I'd like to go back to your house and change into some clean clothes."

Afterwards, Inez gave him a grand tour of some of Nova Scotia. She was the navigator this time and they went inland and north to Trurro then up to New Glasgow where they had lunch and then the coastal route back to Halifax.

Before going home, they picked up the makings for pizza and two bottles of chardonnay wine.

While the pizza cooked, they had a glass of wine and sat in the living room talking. "I'm sure tomorrow we'll have your answer to the document."

There was heavy rain that night and by Monday morning it had blown out to sea and the sun came out hot and humid.

Inside the institute was climatically controlled and they were very comfortable.

Inez began immediately transposing words for the Norwegian symbols. After a half hour she said, "Sweetheart."

"Yeah."

"So far this isn't making much of any sense. Do you suppose this could only be someone's practical joke?"

"I don't think it's a joke," and he read what she had so far. And there it was, "There!" he said excitedly, "No, my love, this isn't a joke and here's the clue. Look," and he pointed to a translated phrase that contained dimple rock.

"Trust me this isn't a joke and we need to finish translating."

Two more paragraphs and there was another phrase, vernal equinox. "Vernal means spring and it happens on March 20th."

"Back up a few words, sweetheart, and it says at first light. Sunrise on the vernal or spring equinox, March 20th."

"And look here, love, two lines down. It says, *straight onward from dimple rock, sun will engulf you.*"

"So on the vernal equinox from the dimple on the rock at sunrise will give us a quadrant to follow. Does it say how far to follow this course?"

"I'm almost at the end. Let me finish, there may be something else."

After a few minutes she said, "I think there's more. It says you do not always have to look up to see the beauty of your surroundings. "I'm guessing whatever there is you will find it on the ground. Maybe another clue?"

"Is there anymore?"

"Two more lines that speaks of rocky ground."

"That's it. It has to be. Listen to this and see how it sounds to you."

"Okay."

215

"From the dimple in the kidney rock on the spring equinox, which is March 20th, at sunrise. The angle from the dimple to the rising sun is the course we must follow to find another rock which we will recognize and there will be another clue. Well?"

"It sounds possible. But I'm confused. You say dimple, dimple rock and now the kidney rock".

"I was going to save this until I could show you as I explain. But I think I'll have to explain now. My 7th great grandparents, in 1770, found this chest under a rock that is shaped like a kidney, and we have always referred to it as the kidney rock. And exactly in the center of the rock is a small dimple."

"Okay, I can understand it better now. You're telling me this chest and document has been in your family for two hundred and thirty years.

"I'll say it again, whoever wrote this was a wizard. It was written as it is so it would never be deciphered by the wrong people."

"See, sweetheart, you are as much a part of this mystery now as I am. Without you this would never have been understood." And on another note he said, "Do you want to hear something else?" and he cupped her cheek in his hands and said, "I love you, Inez Ferguson."

She stood up and hugged him and said, "I was about to say the same to you. I love you. We need to get to Belfast," she said.

"I think if we hurry, we can catch the 6 o'clock return trip."

"What about my car?"

"We leave it for now. I'm sure we'll have to come back to the institute again."

They picked up everything from her office plus the hard copy to both translations, the print out, and then she deleted the information from her computer.

Inez hurriedly packed and Enos locked her car doors. They made it just in time to catch the 6 p.m. ferry to Bar Harbor. And they were able to get a cabin for the night.

The evening meal was served at 8 p.m. and there would be no breakfast. As they ate, she said, "I feel like I'm running away," and then she laughed.

They stayed in the observation lounge until it was too dark to see anything. Then they retired to their cabin.

"These bunks are too narrow for the both of us. I'll take the top bunk. I'm smaller.

"This has been an exciting day, sweetheart." Inez said, "I'm truly in love, we solved the secret and I'm on my way to a new home." Then in another note, "I hope the boat don't sink tonight."

* * *

Bar Harbor was overrun with tourists so they waited to have breakfast in Ellsworth. And they found a waffle shop. "I haven't had waffles since I was a little girl."

"These are better than my mother used to make," Enos said.

An hour later they drove in the long driveway at home. "This is the original house Enig and Innis built in 1770. Of course through the years, as families grew, two additions were added."

Before he had carried their suitcases inside, Inez said, "I want to see this kidney rock."

"It's behind the house."

When she saw all the headstones she asked, "What is this, a shrine?"

"No, during the wars this country has been in, my ancestors would rebury the chest and document under the rock, thinking that if we were ever overrun they would be safe there. Enig and Innis decided to be buried on either side of the rock to discourage anyone from trying to remove it.

"After Fergus and Debra were buried, it was obvious they would be running out of room, so since then everyone has been cremated and the ashes buried with a headstone, to save room."

"It does look like a kidney. Where is the dimple?"

"See if you can find it."

She got down on her hands and knees and she wasn't long finding it. "You know, if there was a little dirt in that no one would ever see it.

"You said Enig and Innis found the chest? How did they just happen to find it under the rock?"

"They were trying to remove it."

"You know, Enos, some time when we're at the institute again we can do a laser ablation and test it in the mass spectrometer to determine the age of the chest and document."

"Would we be allowed to use the equipment?"

"I'm not certified, are you?"

"Yes, we have the equipment in our main office in Bangor. I didn't want to do the tests there because there would be too many questions."

"I understand."

"Let's carry everything inside and I'll show you the house."

Inside she said, "Wow, this is nice. This was built in 1770? Amazing. I love the solid wood walls. I see the safe in the corner, I take it that's where the chest is kept?"

"Yes, I'll open it and put it in." He removed all the family papers and she saw the stacks of money.

"How much money do you keep in there? You don't trust banks."

"Here, this is Enig and Innis' original will. It should explain some for you. This is the family journal, you may also find interesting. While you're reading those, I need to wash some clothes."

He loaded the washing machine and started back to the living room and he suddenly stopped and shouted, "Hey damn! Why didn't I see this before?"

Inez was startled and she said, "What's the matter, sweetheart? Why did you shout?"

"Damn," he said again. "How would you like to find the second clue today, now, instead of waiting for the vernal equinox?"

"How?"

"We have to go back to the rock."

"Now what?"

"This rock is aligned north and south. When the sunrises on the vernal equinox it rises due east. I'll set up my laser transit and align it to the north and swing a ninety degree angle to the east."

"Then with a GPS unit we follow it. Do you have a GPS?" Inez asked.

"Yes."

"What are we waiting for, let's do it." She was just as excited as he was now.

"While you're getting set up, I'll put the chest and papers back in the safe."

"When you have that done, there is a small trenching tool hanging on the wall in the garage."

"I'll find it."

It didn't take him long to set up over the dimple and swing a ninety angle to the east. He then aligned his GPS unit to follow the angle."

Inez went east and he guided her in the correct direction, as far as he could see her in the transit. "Right there, Inez, tie an orange flagging ribbon. Okay hold the ribbon up. Back towards you only a whisper. Too much. Hold it, tie it right there."

She knew what he was doing now. He came up with the GPS and they started trekking due east while watching the ground for something familiar. They had almost reached the property line when Inez hollered, "Here! Here, Enos!" There's a small dimple in this rock. Just like the kidney rock."

"Good eye, sweetheart. Here hold the GPS unit and I'll start digging. He dug down two feet and hit something solid. But it moved. They both were on their stomachs now clearing the dirt away. "It's another chest. We did it!" she said.

"Inez, put up a bunch of ribbon to mark the location."

When she had that done, they started back along the same path following the orange ribbon. "Here, take this in the house and I'll bring the transit in."

Inez had set it on the table and was sitting there looking at it. "Well, that was easy. Let's open it. Go ahead, sweetheart."

The chest was identical to the first chest. And it too held a scroll document. Inez unrolled it. "It is very similar to the other document, only there are fewer symbols to confuse us.

"Where is your computer I'll get started."

He showed her to the computer room, ex-bedroom. "While you're working here, I'll make us a lunch."

Twenty minutes later he had soup and grilled cheese sandwiches. "Lunch is ready."

"Be right out."

As they ate she said, "I should have this one deciphered before this evening."

"How come so fast?"

"Well, I already know the symbols and all I have to do is insert the translation. And there aren't as many this time."

After lunch he said, "Will you be alright here alone for a bit? I need to make a run to town. You probably could work better if I wasn't here."

"I'll be fine."

She went right to work. She didn't know why, but it suddenly was becoming as important for her as it was for Enos, to discover what the secret was hiding.

Enos stopped at the supermarket, the post office and two more stops before returning home. He put the groceries away and left the mail on the table. There was nothing needing his immediate attention.

"Another hour and I'll be done," she hollered from the computer room.

"Would you like a cup of coffee?"

"Yes. Did you get everything done?"

"Yes, I went to the post office and supermarket. We didn't have anything for breakfast. For supper I thought we'd eat at a nice restaurant."

"Sounds good to me. This is good coffee."

"Thank you; it's instant."

"Well, it's still good. I'm almost done."

He stood behind her watching the screen change looking over her shoulder. But not thinking much about the computer or what the document might reveal. He was in love.

"There it's done. All we have to do now is print it."

"We have had a busy day. Let's say we wait until tomorrow to print it."

She stood up and turned to face him. "You know, Inez, the most fascinating thing about this whole search is meeting you. I can't describe how I feel, only that I am so much in love with you. And whether you realize it or not, you have become one of the keepers, a guardian of the family secret. And I never want to lose you." He kissed her lips softly and as their lips were touching he whispered, "I love you, Inez."

"You make me feel so good all over, sweetheart. You make me feel like I really belong and I am so happy."

And then she surprised him when she asked, "Well, are you going to ask me to marry you or not?" They both cracked up laughing.

"I was getting to that," and they both laughed some more and he pulled a ring box out of his pocket and opened it. "Will you marry me, Inez?"

"Yes," and she hugged and kissed his face all over.

As he was sliding the ring on her finger she said, "I never thought I would find divine love like this."

"We have reservations at the Benson Seaside Restaurant for 7 o'clock."

"Then I'd better—we'd better—shower then."

Enos wore a sport coat and tie and Inez wore a pretty summer print dress. When they walked in everyone stopped to look at them. "I feel like we're on display or something," she said.

"I think even women enjoy looking at a beautiful woman."

The maître d' seated them at the window table and said, "Your hostess will be here soon."

"Good evening, folks, I'll be your hostess for the evening. My name is Genell. Would you like something to drink before ordering?"

"Yes a chateau St. Michelle please."

"A very good choice."

While they waited, they looked at the menu. "You know, sweetheart," Inez said, "I like the looks of the buffet."

"Good choice."

Genell was back with the wine and she filled each wine goblet. "Are you ready to order now?"

"Yes, we both would prefer the buffet."

"Good choice. The dinnerware is at the end of the table and I'll return with your silverware."

"I don't know where to start, it all looks so good," Inez said.

They decided on a little of many dishes.

Not one word was spoken about the chest or document. Enos still had a difficult time believing his good fortune when he met Inez. And now less than a week later he had asked her to marry him. There was one thing for certain though, he had never been so happy in his entire life. And he was sure Inez felt the same.

"Everything is so good. I'd like to go back for more, but I think I'll settle for more wine," Inez said.

"Good choice."

It had been a long day and they both were getting sleepy.

"Are you ready to go?" he asked.

"Yes, this wine has made me—well it has stimulated my sexual desires and I can't wait to get home."

Enos left a good tip and thanked the maître d and Genell. And they both almost ran for his pickup.

* * *

As they made love over and over, Inez kept thinking how happy she was. She was making love to the only man she had ever loved, he had asked her to marry him and here in the McFarney house she was feeling truly at home. She couldn't imagine herself any happier. And tonight all of the sexual frustrations she had pent up inside of her were now being released. She truly wanted to please Enos, but at the same time she found it equally important that, for once, her sexual needs, desires and pleasures be fulfilled. And Enos was enjoying every moment.

They were still embraced in each others arms when they woke the next morning.

"Thank you for last night, sweetheart," she said. "That was better than the first time we made love."

"You were fantastic, Inez."

Neither of them mentioned a word about the document until after the breakfast dishes were washed and dried. And without saying a word they drifted to the computer room and Inez began to print out the document.

She printed off two copies and for a few moments they each were silent, then Enos said, "If anyone was to read this, they wouldn't have any idea what was behind it," Enos said.

"I think that was the author's whole point. Just in case it were to fall into the wrong hands," she said.

"Here where it says, ... *you must hurry to follow the sun before all shadows of the vernal sun are gone,* I think it is telling us we must go in the direction of the setting sun on the vernal equinox. If the sun rises due east, then it must set due west."

"And here," Inez said, "It says hurry but watch for a sore

on the kidney. It must refer to the dimple on the kidney rock."

"I think you're right. Let's set up and go find—whatever is waiting for us."

He reset his laser transit and turned the scope exactly 270° west. Inez was already ahead of him with the orange ribbon. The due west course went right though where the old mule barn had once stood. He set his GPS unit to the same course and they started exploring westerly, leaving orange ribbons for a trail.

"What was the distance from the kidney rock before? Did you save it?"

He checked his GPS and said, "It was 733 feet exact."

"How far have we come now?"

"519 feet."

"You're thinking the same thing, I think," he said.

"We're getting close. We are now at 710 feet." They were in a hardwood grove and they had slowed their pace, looking all around them.

At exactly 733 feet they came to a four foot granite ledge wall. "I don't see any rock that looks like a kidney," Inez said.

"Me neither. I'm going to try something. Stand right here and I'm going back on our trail fifty feet."

He checked his GPS to make sure he was on the right 270° heading and then he sighted in to the ledge wall. "Back up a step sweetheart. Okay put your hand on the ledge wall. Extend your hand about three inches. Good right there. Hold it."

"I think I know what you are thinking," and she got down on her knees scanning the wall with her hand in place.

"Here! Here it is! The dimple," she said excitedly.

"It sure is. Good eye. I don't know if I would have seen it."

"What do you think, sweetheart, under the ledge or in front of it?"

"Let's start digging and find out." They were both on their knees now. Inez was digging with her hands.

She brushed the ledge wall with her hand and said, "Look,

another dimple."

"Wait a minute," he measured the distance between the two dimples. "Two feet exact. I think we have to go two feet below the second dimple."

They kept digging and at two feet, "There's a hole or pocket in the ledge," Inez said and she started digging like a woodchuck, sand and gravel being thrown out behind her.

"It is a pocket," Enos said. "We'll have to enlarge this hole if we are going to be able to get to it."

Inez crawled down into the hole. "The pocket is opening larger but I still don't see anything."

"We'll have to keep digging." It was slow work digging with a trenching tool and bare hands. Inez crawled down in the hole again and began pulling dirt out from the pocket. "I see it! I see it Enos!"

"Can you reach it?"

"Yes, I have my hands on it but I need you to pull me out." He pulled her back by her ankles and she was cradling a chest like a baby.

"It looks just like the other two," she said.

"Let's not open it until we're back at the house. Could you see how far the pocket goes back into the ledge?"

"Not much further behind the chest. The chest was resting on a rock or maybe a shelf. I couldn't tell."

"I think we need to find out." He crawled down and with the trenching tool he began removing the sand from the inside pocket.

He worked for several minutes clearing the sand and Inez was pushing it back from the hole. "It looks like the shelf was actually manmade. It looks like it has been cut into the rock." He brushed the sand off with his hand. He crawled out and said, "Do you want to see it?"

"You bet I do, after all of this work," and she crawled back in the pocket.

"How could anyone have cut away the rock and leave it so smooth. We're talking over two hundred years ago," she said.

"What does your geology training tell you?"

"That this pocket and shelf are not natural. Let's hike back to the house."

"What about this hole? Do we bury it or leave it?"

"Let's leave it for now. We may want to come back later."

Enos helped her out of the hole. "You're going to need a shower when we get home."

"I'm filthy, even my hair."

"You take a shower and I'll wash up. Then we'll open the chest."

"Okay, I won't be long," she said.

"Are you hungry?" he hollered from the kitchen.

"Maybe a sandwich and coffee."

"Okay."

She rushed through her shower and walked out into the living room drying off with a towel. She stood there facing Enos toweling her hair dry and said, "How can you so calmly make lunch when probably the greatest mystery ever is sitting there on the table."

He turned around to reply and one look at her with nothing on—well he was speechless.

"Well, aren't you just a little curious?"

"Oh—what?" he was still speechless.

"I think the sandwiches are beginning to burn. I'm going to open the chest."

He removed the grilled cheese sandwiches and the pan of soup and joined her at the table. "Go ahead."

"Just like the other two chests, there is only a scroll."

"Unroll it," he was now standing next to her.

She unrolled it and said, "There are no confusing symbols here. It looks like all of it is the old Scottish brogue. This will be an easy document to translate. I'll scan it and download and start the process. This'll only take a minute."

She draped the towel over the chair and took the document to the computer room. Enos filled their cups with soup and put the sandwiches on plates and set the table, just as Inez came back from the computer room, "The program is running."

She sat down with Enos and hungrily devoured her lunch. "I hope my brothers don't stop by for a visit."

"Why wouldn't you want to see them. Is there friction between you?"

"No—but they might find it interesting to see you."

"How do you mean?"

"You're still in your birthday suit."

They both laughed then and she said, "You know, sweetheart, I am so comfortable around you, it doesn't bother me at all to parade around nude."

"Well—I like it."

"Let's go see if the program has finished," she said.

"We sill have a few minutes to wait. Maybe I'll put some clothes on."

Before she reached the bedroom, Enos said, "The programs has finished. I'll print two copies."

They stood over the computer reading the printout. They both read through it before saying anything. Inez said, "It starts off saying this is the last clue."

"Here's more, halfway between vernal sunrise and sunset, you'll find the high noon sunshine warm and bright. The clue, I think, is halfway between sunrise and sunset.

"Didn't you measure equal distances to both hidden chests?"

"Yes, that would make the center, or halfway between, the kidney rock."

"And here's a depth four feet below.

"I'll get a spade and meet you there," he said.

"How are you going to dig down four feet under the rock

227

without the weight of it settling on top of you?"

"Maybe if we started out here. Dig down four or maybe five feet and then tunnel in under the rock."

"Sounds good. There isn't much room between Innis' grave and the rock."

"It'll be tight."

He started digging, being careful of the grave. It had to be dug big enough, so he could stand in it while digging. "That was the last clue, what do you think we'll find?"

He was down two feet and he stopped to catch his breath and stretch his back muscles. "I don't know. Gold, silver, gems. Or maybe knowledge. Information whoever is responsible for this, wanted the world to know but not until the time was right."

"If it is knowledge—what do you suppose it might be?"

"That scares me. What could it possibly be."

"Do you want me to dig a while?"

"I'm okay."

A half hour later the hole was down five feet. "Not to put a damper on your effort sweetheart, but if the hole is only five feet deep and the chest is four feet how are you going to be able to dig a tunnel?

"Good point. We're going to need a bucket and a rope. You'll find those in the garage."

It was slow digging now. He could only fill the bucket half full in order for Inez to be able to pull it up and empty it. "At least it's good digging."

Two hours later the hole was between seven and eight feet deep. "I think it is deep enough now and I'm going to start tunneling."

"Be careful sweetheart."

He only had to go maybe four feet at the most to be under the center of the rock. His spade hit something. "I hit something. I think it's another chest. Just like the other three. A little more work and I think I can pull it out."

He had to work it back and forth to free it. "I've got it." He passed it up to Inez.

"I think you are going to have to help me out of here."

Once out of the hole he said, "I think we better fill the hole in so the rock doesn't settle." Inez set the chest down and started back filling. Enos went after another spade in the garage.

"The chest isn't heavy so I'm assuming there isn't any gold or silver in it. You take the chest in the house and I'll put the spades back."

When Enos came back inside the house, Inez was sitting at the table staring at the chest. "Sit down, sweetheart. We need to talk."

He sat and said, "Okay."

"Before you say anything, I want you to hear me out." He nodded his head yes. "I think we should wait before opening this chest. From the weight of it, I think we can rule out any gold, silver or precious gems. That only leaves knowledge. Knowledge, that once we have it, we'll be the only ones in the world to have it."

"Things will change around here, once we release whatever knowledge this chest contains. I want to get married before then and I still need to go back to the institute and clean out my desk and personal items and tender my resignation." She was silent then looking at Enos.

"I think I'm okay with that. I don't think if we wait a little longer it'll make any difference."

Inez breathed a sigh of relief.

"Which comes first? The wedding or the institute?" he asked. "And what do you want for a wedding?"

"The aunt who helped raise me after my folks died moved back to Glasgow and she was the only family I had. You have two brothers and a sister and their families; maybe a ceremony here with the family."

"Okay, how about Sunday morning. Then Monday morning we take the ferry to Halifax."

* * *

The caterers were the first to arrive and then they left. Then Enos' sister Rachel and her husband David and their two kids, then Reverend Hollis and his wife. Then the two brothers and their wives and kids. Inez looked beautiful in her new dress.

After they were married, Paul went for a walk out back to the family cemetery and saw where Enos and Inez had dug up the ground beside the kidney rock.

"You digging under the rock brother?" Paul asked.

"Nah, the frost had pushed a rock up through the sod and I dug it up, to get rid of it." Inez heard the lie and smiled.

Reverend Hollis came over to say goodbye to Inez. "Mrs. McFarney, this is a very nice family you have married into. After things have settled for you after the wedding, maybe you and your husband might consider joining our church. What faith do you follow?"

"It's called Eckankar," she replied.

"That's funny. I have never heard of it before. How is it different?"

"It's a path of Spiritual Freedom, Reverend Hollis."

"That sounds interesting. I'll have to look into it."

"Reverend Hollis, you can go online and find an introduction."

"I will, I'll do that. And good luck to you and your husband, Mrs. McFarney."

After everyone had left, Enos hugged and kissed his wife and said, "I love you, Mrs. McFarney."

"I like how that sounds."

That evening, they spread out on the table the first three documents. "All three scrolls appeared to be made from the same material, "Inez said.

"As do all four chests. They all are identical."

"The writing on all three is quite exquisite. Every letter on all three documents is exactly alike. Almost like they were printed. I wonder how old these really are?"

"I really think we should take the first chest and document and see if we could do some laser ablation tests on them to find out how old they are."

"Can we get into that part of the institute?"

"I know the person to ask once we are there."

* * *

Mr. and Mrs. Enos McFarney arrived in Halifax, Nova Scotia, at 2:30 p.m. Monday afternoon and went straight to her house.

"I'll call Professor Jack Clifford."

"That didn't take long."

"He said he was planning on being in his office at 8 a.m."

"How much are you moving home?"

"Some pictures, clothes, personal items. The furniture came with the house."

"Maybe we should go to Kmart and get some travel containers."

"While you're doing that, I'll start putting together what I want to take."

"How many containers?"

"Six should be enough."

Before they went to bed that night, Inez had everything packed in the containers, except for clothes she would need.

At 8 a.m. Tuesday morning, Inez knocked on Professor Clifford's office door. "Come in, Inez."

"Professor Clifford, I'd like you to meet my husband Enos McFarney."

"Pleased to meet you. Now what can I do for you?"

"We have two items we would like laser ablation tested and also tested in the mass spectrometer. We are looking for type of material and age. My husband is a geologist for the USGS and he is certified to run the test if you do not have the time," Inez said.

"I know the USGS has the equipment to make these tests, why not use their instruments?"

"I'll answer that indirectly, Professor. But before we start, we must have your signature on this non-disclosure agreement."

"You have my interest," and he signed the agreement. "Now what would you like me to test?"

Enos removed the chest from his travel bag and removed the scroll document. Professor Clifford looked at the document and said, "And am I correct in assuming you have already translated this, Inez?"

"Yes, Professor Clifford, I have. We need to know what the material of each is and age. We are trying to discover where these two originated."

"This document looks and feels like vellum." Then he handled the chest looking at the composition. "This, I'm not so certain. Can you tell me a little more about it?"

"My 7th great grandparents found this behind their house buried under a rock. This was in 1770."

"Wow, you certainly have my interest now. Let's get started. We'll start with the laser ablation, it's inductive coupled plasma uses both the mass spectroscopy and the optical emission spectroscopy techniques, and is very reliable."

After a few minutes, Clifford said, "There, now the computer will have to search through its data banks. I'll start the same tests on the document.

"This is remarkable penmanship; so exact. I'm also going to sample the ink."

Those samples were loaded into another computer. "Now all we have to do is wait," Clifford said

Ten minutes later the first computer signaled it had finished its search and Clifford removed the printout. "This cant' be. It just can't be," he said again.

"What's the problem, Professor Clifford?" Enos asked.

"There is no known element. It is a composite of five

elements, but those are not known."

"And the age, Professor?"

"More than five thousand years. What in hell do you have?"

"That's why we are here, Professor," Inez said.

While they were talking about the chest results, the second computer had finished its search. "I guess this doesn't surprise me. It says the document material is a composite, much like vellum. And the age is the same, more than five thousand years. And the ink is human blood."

"Now I need to do two additional tests. And these two I will insist just to prove this is not a hoax. I hope you understand. I want a DNA sample from each of you, to compare to the ablation sample."

Enos and Inez looked at each other and they both nodded their head in agreement.

Clifford took both ablation samples and the computer had its answer in only a few short minutes. "Now this is interesting. I don't suppose either one of you were alive five thousand years ago."

"Not hardly, Professor."

"Well, your two DNA samples do not match, but there are familial signatures. Only a few. And more surprising, both of your DNA signatures have also familial signatures with the blood on the document. Not a complete signature. Only trace familial signatures. I would have to say that you both are related to whoever wrote this."

The professor picked the document up looking at it and said, "Some of this is old-style Scottish brogue and the symbols are Norwegian. You had me sign a non-disclosure agreement; now I would certainly like to know more about this."

"Do you understand now why we had you sign the agreement?"

"Yes."

They told the professor everything except that they now

had the last chest in their possession. "Now, Professor Clifford, there is one more thing I'd like you to do for us."

"And what is that?"

"We would like you to write out a report of your findings today with your office letterhead and signed. There will be a time—and not too far off—when the world press will want, will require, positive proof of what we have. And there may be some more testing required."

"I'll do that right now."

"You wait here, sweetheart, I'm going to my office for my personal things," Inez said.

First, Inez typed a letter of resignation and emailed it to the faculty office. Then she went through her electronic files and discs and put everything in a box and returned to Professor Clifford's office.

The professor was just handing Enos the results of his examinations. "I hope you'll keep me informed."

"We will; you can count on it."

"We have plenty of time, do you want to leave this evening sweetheart?" Enos asked.

"Yes, I can't wait to get home."

They loaded all of her packed containers in the pickup and had time left for a good meal before boarding the ferry.

It was a warm afternoon and they found a table in the open café overlooking the harbor. They had cheeseburgers and coffee. They had been pretty quiet since leaving the institute; not wanting to think about the implications of the test results. Enos said, "So how are you enjoying your honeymoon so far?"

Inez was just taking a sip of her coffee and when Enos asked that she started to laugh and she spit up her coffee onto her plate. Then she really began to laugh. Now Enos was laughing, too.

"Well, it isn't what I always thought my honeymoon would be, but we had to come."

"I promise when this is all behind us we'll take the honeymoon to the south sea island of your choice."

"I'll work on it."

* * *

They drove both of their vehicles onboard the ferry and secured the chest and document in his pickup.

They had wine on the observation deck while talking about anything except the test results.

It was 3 a.m. when the ferry arrived in Bar Harbor, and they drove home while there was very little traffic on the roads. They arrived an hour later, and lay on top of the bed without undressing.

They were both filled with too much apprehension to rest for long. "We might as well get up sweetheart and see what the new chest has to say," Inez said.

"We might as well. We sure aren't going to get any rest until we do."

"What time did we lay down, sweetheart?" Inez asked.

"A little after 3 o'clock."

"I didn't think I had slept at all. How about you?"

"Not that I remember."

"Look at the clock," she said.

"Can't be. That says we were lying down for more than four hours."

"Weird."

"You can say that again," he said.

"Do you want breakfast before or after?"

"Before—after we might not feel like eating."

"Scrambled eggs and bacon?"

"Sounds good."

While Inez was cooking breakfast, he unloaded the pickup and for now he put everything in the living room. "Breakfast is ready."

"Some day when we have time, I'd like to inquire at the

University in Orono about a teaching job."

"That would be good for you."

"Breakfast is done, sweetheart. I'll put the dishes in the sink for now and you bring out the chest and I'll be right in."

Enos opened the safe and brought the chest out and set it on the coffee table in the living room and he waited for Inez.

They sat on the couch staring at the chest. "This may sound silly, but I'm a little afraid what we might find," she said.

"Would we be better off if we don't look and reburied it?"

"I don't know. It's just I'm afraid what the document might have to say."

"Do you think we were picked at random to discover the secret and understand what it says?" he asked trying to comfort his wife.

"Not on your life. I think this has been our destiny since birth and that would explain how we fell so much in love with each other.

"Well are we going to open it or just sit here and stare at it?" he asked.

She took a deep breath and said, "Let's do it."

"Okay, I'll open the chest and you take the scroll out. You are the linguist."

"Go ahead," she held her breath.

He opened the chest and there just like the other three was the scroll. She took it out and before unrolling it she looked at Enos. He nodded his head.

"It's all old Scottish brogue and no symbols at all. This should be an easy document to translate. Do you want me to do it now?"

"Might as well."

She scanned it into her computer and started running the program.

While Inez was busy, he put the chest under a bright light and then he used a magnifying glass and went over every inch of the chest. "What are you looking for?"

"Answers."

"Did you find anything?"

"Not a thing."

Twenty minutes later the printer started working. She printed two copies and they sat down to read.

Congratulations, you made the search to end. No idea who you are, but if you are reading this, it is clear you level understanding was high enough to understand clues in the three scrolls.

I also sure your science is at a level making possible to translate documents. You understand, it had to be to prevent any undeserving entity from discovering this document. The wrong people would use knowledge within for own benefit.

I regret never knowing who is reading this. And I not disclose who I am, not important. Now you are ready to learn what written within? Of course you are or you not have solved mystery.

This world most beautiful and bountiful in all universe. People will destroy it. But I get to that later.

The Great Architect not create this world on random whim. Everything is as supposed to be. Molten earth began to cool releasing from rock oxygen and hydrogen making water to sustain life. This world still making water.

The world lives, breaths and grows. The time will come too many kicking sleeping lion and lion will bite back.

World will see cycles of lush forest green savannahs and waving fields of grain. Some day savannahs will dry and wind blow sand cover lakes and rivers and villages. Cycle will change and savannahs will grow green again.

Civilizations and empires will grow, expand only to disappear, make room for another. Continents will flourish and then destroy. Empires will fight and invade other countries. The world goes into era of unrest and turbulence and millions will die. New weapons will be created making easier to kill more people.

Oil will be discovered below in depths that will change the world. Nation will fight nation for this oil. Life will prosper from the discover. But as anything newly discovered for human use, eventually will be discovered negative side effects.

Greatest energy will come from material as bright and powerful as sun. But it too must be learned how to use safely. But once learned it will power the entire world safely and without dirting air.

Before this comes to be empires will use this power energy against enemies. Cities will be destroyed and whole countries millions will die. An island nation will disappear. Much of all coastal regions will change. Continent in western hemisphere will be divided and much of west coast will disappear. Land where this document was found will be safe. That is why this location was chosen.

In nature world when specie becomes too many, many must die to make room for those who survive to procreate and expand in understanding. Same is true in people world. These events already started because too many people no longer responsible. Only care about ownself not other people.

Some will heed warning, many will not and many will go.

"This is quite profound," Enos said.

"I can see it happening now what is said about people not being responsible," Inez said. "All you have to do is look around."

"Everywhere you go. I agree with you," Enos said. "Shall we read on?"

Democracy will be a good form of government. So long as people are responsible. When not, weak groups will pass laws to protect themselves. Slowly then tyranny will replace democracy, people will need strong leader to look up to. Not to worry tyranny will also vanish in time.

New races will make an appearance from time to time. Some will stay and a few will vanish. But they bring new ideas and procedure in governing.

Before that happens, top to bottom poles will shift. Gradual shift not have to worry. If flip-flop ocean surges over much land taking many lives. This is only natural occurrence.

Everything, good or bad comes in cycles. This world is living being.

Man will learn to live under ocean. In warm tropical water. South of equator, science develops extremely strong durable metal that is clear like glass. Becomes popular and many people choose to live, only drawback is must be built in warm water no tectonic movement or bad wind driven storms.

Man will also build dwellings on moon. Water is found under surface. Two new elements are discovered also which is used in metal dwellings under ocean. Moon will provide base for travel to Mars. Man will eventually visit but unable to sustain living there and is soon forgotten.

There are two continents that were submerged cause they kicked the lion too much. They each will rise again. One in the east and the other in the west, north of the equator. As these two rise from deep ocean there will be high water levels everywhere. Many people will die.

Years later there will be fighting who see which empire will control these new land masses. But of course that is long time from when you are reading this.

In years to come, many advancements in health and technology. There will come an era when machines used for travel no longer will dirty air. This will be marvelous era. A good time to be alive.

I could go on and on and probably bore you to death. My point is this. This earth world is a living, breathing, entity and if people do not become more responsible and stop blaming everyone else for their problems and stop kicking the lion—well then, some of these catastrophic events will happen sooner than they are intended to be. Man must learn that their actions will stir the angry lion.

You have no idea who I am nor I you. But I do know, because you are reading this document you are of good character and morally guided. It is up to you now what you do with this. The world needs to understand they can not continue kicking the lion and blaming others for their own problems. Because if they do, the consequences can be quite severe.

It is up to you now what you are going to do with this information. As I said it is up to you.

Enos and Inez just sat there in silence looking at each other. Finally she said, "Wow."

"You can say that again."

"Do you feel the weight of the whole world on our shoulders?" she asked.

"Something like that. A great responsibility has been given to us."

"What do we do with this?" she asked.

"From the document, I think we are expected to tell the world to Stop KICKING THE LION."

Made in the USA
Columbia, SC
27 February 2025

54502747R00133